Buddhist Folk Tales from Ancient Ceylon

Buddhist Folk Tales
from Ancient Ceylon

Translated and Compiled by Dick de Ruiter

Binkey Kok Publications – Havelte/Holland

Buddhist Folk Tales from Ancient Ceylon
Translated and Compiled by Dick de Ruiter
First published by Binkey Kok Publications

An edition of Binkey Kok Publications – Havelte/Holland
www.binkeykok.com
e-mail info@binkeykok.com

ISBN 90-74597-86-6

Edited by Valerie Cooper
Cover design and layout by Jaap Koning

Contents

Introduction

At the end of the nineteenth and the beginning of the twentieth century, when India and Sri Lanka (Ceylon) were under British rule, the stories from this book were for the first time recorded by European authors like Victor Fausböll, Lord Robert Chalmers, Edward Cowell, H. T. Francis, E. J. Thomas, Marie Shedlock, and the Rhys Davids (*The Buddhist Birth Stories*, London, 1880).

Tthese tales are hundreds of years old, possibly even older than the time when the *Shakya*, the Buddhist doctrine, was founded. Some of them were probably transmitted to India from other countries. Others are obviously of a Buddhist origin. However, all of these *jatakas* (teaching stories) have been assimilated into the oldest known tradition of the Buddhist doctrine.

They have been adapted, however, according to the changing times, and, depending on the region, local singularities were also added. The stories were passed on orally, which is the reason why, for example, a story from Northern India may be the same as one from Ceylon, but their contents and names might differ considerably.

The Buddhist monks on the island of Ceylon told the tales in this book to the common people. On warm full moon nights, before the holy day, they were told in Sinhalese, and the verses often were sung to the people in Pali, the sacred language of the Buddhists, and then translated into Singalese. This tradition goes back at least three hundred years. The monks sang the jatakas verses in a special tonality, which to our ears resembles the age-old Gregorian chants, but blended with the elegiac, typically Eastern tinge of intonation, with the veena, the Indian lute, as a traditional accompaniment.

The earliest of the two "chronicles" from Ceylon, the *Dipavamsa*, originates from the fifth century A.D., while the later one, the circa sixth-century *Mahavamsa*, actually has much older origins. Many parts of it have been lost, so we never can tell if we have the complete stories in our hands.

Today these stories are still being passed on, from generation to generation, as "expedient means"—a mild form of popular religious education, or at least a moral teaching of the Buddhist axioms. They continue to find a willing ear among the people of Ceylon.

In this translation I have maintained the original composition as it was passed on in the Pali language. That is to say, the jataka begins with the occasion, usually someone (often a monk) who is consulting the Master about his problem or an odd incident. Next, they sit down with the congregation and the Master begins narrating his parable about a life from a distant past, in which he himself is playing a key role, as a trader, a caravan-leader, a bandit, a hare, an ape, or an elephant, which clarifies the moral inherent in the events. The third part is the closing sentence, telling the current names of the leading figures of the past.

The stories tell about the lives of the Bodhisattva, meaning the Buddha before his enlightenment. One of the recurring items in the tales is the Master uttering poetic choruses. These would be sung by the monks relating the jataka. No doubt, in their original forms, these are very beautiful, but the style is difficult to keep in translation. The original tales contained many repetitions, mainly in these verses, presumably in order to better impress the message upon the listeners, mostly simple peasants or young Buddhist students. These repetitions I have left out of my translation, because in written form they are of little use.

Another kind of repetition is harder to explain. Many of the stories of the Bodhisattva have the same opening: "A long time ago, when Brahmadatta was reigning at Benares, the Bodhisattva was born as. . ." Well, this Brahmadatta must have reigned for an extraordinarily long time, if all of those lives were lived during his reign! No doubt there is another, symbolic explanation of this.

The subject of many tales is the eternal attempts of *Devadatta*—you might say a "fallen angel"—to kill and destroy the Bodhisattva and his works of merit. And of course, in the stories Devadatta is always getting the worst of it. It is the metaphor of our own eternal struggle between good and evil inside ourselves.

So, as much as possible, I observed the original ways of expression in English and Sanskrit, and the parlance may seem somewhat inflated and old-fashioned, just like it was in centuries past. I feel it is important not to bastardize this original use of language—after all, it was the usual way of expression in those days.

Noteworthy in these jatakas is the woman's role. Although in the doctrine of Hinayana Buddhism a woman could not be a Buddhist teacher herself, she plays a role as often as the men, and she is ascribed a will of her own and a position in society—something that was is very special in those days. Sometimes she appears as a ruler or consort, overpowering husband, son, daughter-in-law, or empire; she is mother to man as the weaker half; and the man acknowledges his impotence to fathom her (so much the worse for his own wisdom, which is subordinate to hers); she will save his life; she will choose her partner. . .

The most important message readers can distill from these parables, as an extract of Buddhist ideas, is the individual soul's strength to survive, through many lives, although a dogmatically Buddhist practitioner will probably deny this.

The Buddha himself used two ways of teaching: the first was meant to be for the masses, using more popular terms and narration; the other was meant for the more advanced practitioner, the monk, to whom ordinary terms, like man (the self, the soul), woman, me and you, house, and chariot, had another meaning, hinting to what was happening in the "other realms."

Just before he left the world, the founder of the Shakya gospel himself said it like this: "Not one single Bodhisattva ever had the fist of the teacher (sometimes open, then again closed); He will only hand down all He knows."

It is my hope that you will be inspired by the age-old, timeless jewels offered in this book. For me they have been an exquisite inspiration.

> *He of gladsome heart,*
> *the man who's joyful in mind,—*
> *he makes goodness come to be,*
> *to win the goal he seeks;*
> *he in due course may succeed*
> *in bringing ev'ry hindrance to an end.*[1]

– 1 –
The Sandy Road
«Vannupatha-jataka»

In the sandy desert, the digging never ended. . .

This lesson the Blessed One taught while living in Savatthi. The story is about a monk who gave up effort.

The story goes that when the Tathâgatha[2] was living in Savatthi,[3] a man from the Savatthi family went to the Jetavana monastery to hear the Master teaching the Dhamma.[4] Five years had passed since he had been initiated, and he had learned a lot. He had been training himself in methods of insight and received from the Teacher a subject of exercise, which appealed to him, so he went into retreat in the middle of the forest, striving to get results. During the whole rainy season he trained very earnestly, but he did not attain any spiritual progress.

Then he thought, "There are four kinds of people who the Master has taught; among them I was meant to attain the highest grade. But I do not think I shall make it in this lifetime. What am I doing here in the forest? I shall go back to the Teacher and contemplate the blissful Buddha-body and listen to the honey-sweet teachings of the Dhamma." And so he returned to the Jetavana monastery.

His companions and messmates said, "Reverend Sir, we thought the Master assigned to you an exercise, and that you had decided to practice in seclusion. But now you are back and actively take part in the community. What has happened? Did you attain the high end of your Dhamma duties? Are you now past the wheel of rebirth?"

"Brothers, I have attained neither this nor that. I am to become someone who did not succeed. I came back because I gave up effort."

"But Reverend Sir, there should not be any reason for that, to give up now, after you had already left behind the world of the Teacher, who is himself mighty in effort. Come, we shall bring you to the Tathâgatha." And together they went to see the Master.

When they stood before him, he said, "Monks, you have taken a brother who is unwilling, what has happened to him?"

"Reverend Sir, this monk had left behind the world of religion, with so many distractions, to work in seclusion in the forest, but now he has returned because he gave up effort."

Then the Teacher said, "Is it true, monk, that you have given up your efforts?"

"It is true, O blessed one," he answered.

"How is it, brother, when you had already given up the world and desire, to live in seclusion, and do your utmost, that now you have given up? Was it not you who were full of effort in the past? Was it not on account of what you did on your own, that when five hundred carts were stranded in the desert, men and oxen could obtain water and were able to survive? Why have you, of all people, given up now?"

Thereupon the monk felt somewhat encouraged again. But when the monks heard what the Teacher had said, they begged the Blessed One, "O Reverend Sir, it is now made clear to us that this monk lost his courage, but what you are saying about what he did in the past we never knew; only to your omniscience it was clear. Tell us about it!"

"Well then, brothers, listen!" And the Blessed One asked for their full attention and revealed what had happened in a past life.

৯০

Long ago, when Brahmadatta reigned at Benares, the *Bodhisattva*, born to the family of a caravan leader, had grown up, and he was traveling about with five hundred carts, doing trade.

One day he was passing through a sandy desert of over sixty leagues. The desert sand was so fine that when you grasped it with the fist, it would slip right through your fingers. From the moment of sunrise the sand became burning hot—no one could walk on it. That is why the caravan was packed with oil, wood, and rice, and traveled only by night. In the morning they would place the carts in a circle, and spread a tent over the top. After they would eat at sunrise, they would spend the day sitting or sleeping in the shadow. At sunset, after a timely meal, and when the ground was cooler again, they yoked the carts and moved on.

The navigation happened the same way as at sea: they needed a "land pilot," with his knowledge of the stars, to guide the caravan safely through the desert. On that occasion too, the caravan leader guided his carts through that endless desert. And when they had been going for sixty miles already, he said, "Still one more night to go, then we shall reach the other side of the desert." So after supper he ordered that the remaining firewood be thrown away, and they took off to trek through the last bit of barren desert. The navigator spread a mat on the lead cart, and lied down to watch the stars and give directions now and then. But because he had been going for so many days without sleep, his eyes became heavy and finally he fell asleep, unaware of the fact that the oxen were slowly turning around and moving back the way they had come, deeper into the desert again. The oxen went on all night. When dawn was breaking, the land pilot suddenly woke up, looked at the stars, and yelled, "Turn the carts, the other way around, the other way around!" While the caravan turned, and the carts were drawn back in line, the sun rose above the horizon. To their dismay, the men saw that they were standing on the very same spot they had left last night. "We have thrown away all our wood and used up all our water; now we are doomed!" they said, abashed. After the carts were unpacked and placed in a circle once more, and they pulled the awning over them, they could only lie down and wail, each by their own cart.

The Bodhisattva thought, "If I give up now, we are really lost." He looked around; it was not really hot yet and he saw a little patch of dabba grass. He thought, "If grass is growing here, it means there is water, somewhere down there." So he gathered some spades and had the men dig at that spot. When one of the diggers struck a rock, they all gave up. But the Bodhisattva thought, "Beneath this rock there should be water." He jumped into the hole, crouched on the rock, and cocked his head to see if he could hear something. And indeed, he heard the sound of water flowing down there!

He came out of the hole and said to a young attendant, "*Tata*,[5] if you give up all effort now, we shall all be lost. Do not give up now! Take this sledgehammer and shatter that rock!" While all the others had already returned to their carts, the boy obeyed and did what the Bodhisattva had said, and hit the rock hard. The rock broke into two pieces and fell below, so the water could come up without obstruction. A spout of water rose as high as a palm tree, and all the men could drink and bathe. Then they chopped up the spare axles of the carts for firewood, cooked rice, and ate as much as they could. They gave the oxen their food and when the sun was setting they planted a flag by the well, a place where later a new oasis would flourish. Then they took off to their destination at the end of the desert.

They sold their goods at double and fourfold profit and, laden with other wares, they turned home.

As long as they lived they never forgot the way they survived this trip. And the Bodhisattva, working merit, went according to his deeds. The Rightly Enlightened One then spoke these words:

> In the sandy desert, the digging never ended,
> Along the way they found water.
> SSo the wise man, with effort and strength
> Unrelenting, will work until he finds peace of heart.

The Teacher concluded this Jataka: "This monk who has given up effort now was the young attendant who never gave up; his current companion monks were his fellow travelers, but the caravan leader was just I."

– 2 –
The Divine Nature
«Deva-dhamma-jataka»

Those who are modest and discrete. . . the world calls divine

When living at the Jetavana monastery, the Blessed One told this tale about a monk who had many possessions.

The story goes that a landowner, who was living in Savatthi, decided to say goodbye to the world after his wife died. He had a hermitage built for himself, with a fireplace and a storage area. He ordered that this storage area be filled with butter and rice and other food, and every day he sent for servants to prepare his meals. And his monk outfit was also outstanding: he had a garment for the daytime and another for the night. He had this hermitage built on the outskirts of the area belonging to the monastery.

One day, when he had hung out his washed clothing and bed linen to dry, monks from the country came by; they had been on a long and tiring journey and were looking for a place to stay for the night. Seeing the clothes hanging they asked, "Whose clothes are these?!"

The monk answered, "These are mine, reverends."

"Reverend, this over garment, all this underwear, and also all this bedding—all only yours?"

"Yes, only mine," was his answer.

"Reverend, only three garments are permissible according to the Blessed One; and yet you, who have entered the Order of a so-little-demanding Buddha, still you are so laden with clothing! Come on, we shall take you with us to the One of the Ten-Powers."[6]

When the Teacher saw them he said, "Why, monks, are you bringing a monk to me against his own will?"

"Reverend Sir, this monk owns many goods and conveniences."

"Is this true, monk, what they say?"

"It is true, Blessed One," he replied.

"But why are you a man who owns so much? Didn't I often recommend wishing little and being satisfied with what you have?" When he heard the Master's words he said, peevishly, "Well then, if I go like this, will it be all right?" And he tossed aside his robe, so he stood only in his undergarment.

The Master, coming to his support, said, "Was it not you, monk, who of old were a seeker after modesty and discretion? And although you were a water demon in that life, did you not live for twelve years in that quest? Then why do you now, while having left the world in such a revered Order as the Buddha's, lay aside your cloak for all to see, while feeling no modesty or discretion?"

Thereupon he submitted, bowed humbly before the Master, donned his cloak, and sat down.

Then the Blessed One revealed what had happened in a past life.

In the past, Brahmadatta was king at Benares in the kingdom of Kasi. At that time, the Bodhisattva was born as a child of the chief queen,[6] and was named Mahingsása. When he could walk, another son was born to the king; and his name was Chanda (Moon). But when this child could also walk, the mother died.

Then the king appointed another wife as his chief queen. She was very sweet and charming to the king. She also gave birth to a son, and they named him Surya (Sun).

When the king saw this son, he was very pleased and grateful, and he said, "Dear wife, I am so happy with this son that I shall grant you a wish."

The queen answered that she would rather save it for when she could put it to best use.

When her son had grown up, she said to her king, "Lord, I remind you of the wish you granted me when my son was born. My wish is: Let my son be your successor, as ruler of your *kingdom.*"

But the king emphatically refused, saying, "I do have two other sons, bursting with energy, who have just as many rights as he has; so no, I cannot give my kingdom to one son only."

But the woman kept on begging, so he thought, "She might have something evil in mind toward my other two sons," and he sent for his sons. He told them: "*Tatas*, when Surya was born, his mother was allowed a wish, and now she wishes the whole kingdom for him. I do not want to grant him this like that. The woman obviously has no respect; it might be that she devises evil against you. So it is better for you to temporarily withdraw into the forest. When I am gone, you may rule the country that is ours." Weeping and sobbing, he kissed them affectionately on their foreheads and allowed them to leave. They saluted their father and left the palace. But Surya, while he was playing in the courtyard, saw them leaving, and when he learned what their father had told them, he said, "I shall go with you." And so he joined his brothers, and the three of them went into the woods.

They entered the mountainous Himalaya region. The Bodhisattva left the road and sat down beneath a tree. He was very tired and begged Surya, "*Tata* Surya, would you go down to that lake over there? Bathe, drink, and fill some lotus leaves with water so that we, too, may drink."

However, this lake was possessed by a water demon from Vessavana, who had told him: "You can have and eat everyone who comes to the lake, except those who know what is divine; these people you will have to leave alone." From that day on, the demon asked everyone who came to the lake if they knew what was divine, and he ate everyone who could not answer the question.

When Surya went down to the lake, the demon seized him immediately and asked, "Do you know what is divine?"

"Chanda and Mahingsása are divine," Surya said.

"You are wrong," the demon told him, "You do not know what is divine," and took Surya captive in the demon's lake abode.

The Bodhisattva, who realized that Surya have been gone too long, asked Chanda to go and have a look. The demon seized him, too, and asked again: "Do you know what is divine?"

"Yes, I know," said Chanda. "The four corners of the firmament are divine."

But that was also the wrong answer, so he was also caught in the lake.

When Chanda also did not return, the Bodhisattva thought, "Something troubling must have happened to them," and he, too, went down to the lake. He saw the footprints disappearing into the lake and thought, "This lake must be haunted by some demon." He drew his sword, grabbed his bow, and waited. The water demon, who saw that the Bodhisattva did not step into the lake, transformed into a forester and said to the Bodhisattva, "Young fellow, your journey must have exhausted you. Why don't you enter the lake to bathe, drink, eat the lotus stalks, dress up with these beautiful lotus flowers, and then leave all refreshed and energized?"

The Bodhisattva knew the forester was actually a demon and said, "You have caught my two young brothers."

"Yes, I did," answered the demon.

"Why?"

"Because I seize everyone who comes to this lake."

"What? Do you get them all?"

"Only those who can tell me what is divine may escape; the others are for me."

"Would you not want to know what actually is divine?"

The demon said: "Yes, I would."

"If you would, I shall tell you about it."

"All right, tell me; I am listening."

"I want to tell you about those divine things, but my limbs are so tired," said the Bodhisattva.

So the demon bathed the Bodhisattva, gave him food and drink, covered him with flowers, sprinkled perfumes on his body, and spread a seat for him in an elegant pavillion at the edge of the lake.

The Bodhisattva sat down and made the demon sit at his feet, while he recited this strophe:

Those who are modest and discrete,
In things that are of pure intent—
The holy men, the loved ones—
These the world calls divine.

When the demon heard these sincere teachings, he was pleased and he said to the Bodhisattva, "Wise man, I am very happy with you. I shall give back one of your brothers; which one will it be?"

"Bring the young one," answered the Bodhisattva.

"Wise man, you know exactly how to tell what is divine, but you do not act like this."

"What do you mean?"

"For some reason you chose the younger brother instead of the elder, and I shall not do this if the elder is to blame."

"I know what is divine, demon, but I am also acting accordingly. It was because of this boy that we had to move into this forest; it was because of this younger brother that his mother asked our father to give him the whole kingdom. And because our father refused to grant her this wish and told us to go and live in the woods for a while, this boy has come with us. If later we shall have to say, 'He was devoured in the forest by a demon,' no one will believe us. That is why I am begging you, out of fear of being blamed, to give back my younger brother."

"Very good, very well, wise man! You know what is divine and you act accordingly!"

The demon was pleased and applauded the Bodhisattva, and then gave him back both his brothers.

Then the Bodhisattva said to him, "Because of the bad things you did in the past you were reborn as a sprite, and you are eating the flesh and blood of others. So now you are still doing evil and like this you will never be released from hell and the wheel of rebirth. Why don't you just stop doing these evil things and try to do good?" And he managed to persuade the demon and teach him to do good.

After he had been living there with the sprite as an educator for quite some time, one day he read in the stars that his father had died. And, together with the demon, he returned to Benares.

There he took the responsibility of the kingdom, making Chanda viceroy and Surya his general. Moreover, he sought a pleasant place for the demon to abide, so that he got the best garlands, the best flowers, and the best food. He arranged that he be taken care of in every way, so the demon became a good spirit.

And the Bodhisattva ruled righteously, always living up to his promise.

When the Master had told this story, he concluded his teaching in this jataka with: "In those days, the monk of many goods was the water demon, Ananda was Surya, Sariputta was Chanda, and the elder brother, Mahingsása, was just I."

– 3 –
The Banyan Deer
«Nigrodha-miga-jataka»

It is better to die near the banyan
Than to be alive with the branch.

This the Teacher taught when residing at the Jetavana monastery, about the mother of the elder, Kumara-Kassapa.

The story goes that she was the daughter of a rich and prominent merchant from Rajagaha; she was virtuous, had no interest whatsoever in worldly matters, and she was in her last stage here on earth. Like a clear and shining light in a jar, she was, radiating the essence of a true saint. From the moment she attained self-realization7 she found no more joy in her work at home, and in her desire to leave the world she told her parents, "Dear ones, my heart does not find any joy in life here at home. I desire to leave this world behind and go to the Buddha religion, which leads onwards to the spheres beyond. Let me go to be ordained."

But her parents objected: "Dear one, what are you talking about? We are a very wealthy family and you are our only daughter! You cannot just go and leave the world behind!"

And although she repeatedly asked, they would give no permission.

Then she thought, "So be it! But after I have married into another family, I shall persuade my husband and then finally leave this world behind."

When she grew up she was married into another family and lived in that house as a devoted wife, virtuous and affectionate. And in due time she became pregnant, although she did not know this.

In the city where she was living there was a big festival. All the citizens took a day off and celebrated exuberantly. The city was richly decorated like a deva city.[8] But the woman did not join the party, not even when the festival was at its highlight. She neither anointed nor adorned her body, but went about in her everyday attire. Then her husband said to her, "Dearest one, the whole city is having a party, but you do not even dress up."

She had rehearsed her answer already many times: "My husband, this body of mine is adorned with thirty two corpses[10]— what good will it do to adorn it? This body truly is neither deva-created nor Brahma-created; it is not made of gold or jewels or yellow sandalwood; it was not born out of lotus flowers or lilies, nor is it filled with ambrosial balsam. No, it has been bred in corruption, the product of a mother and a father; it is something that wears and wastes away, in dissolution and destruction, fit for the graveyard, a product of craving, source of sorrows, basin of lamentation, abode of diseases, receptacle of cramped movements, foul within, foul without, sweating, dwelling of vermin and worms, farer to the charnel house, ending in death... Son of the house, what shall I move about now adorning this frame? Is that not something like painting the outside of a muck-filled sink?"

When the merchant's son heard what she said, he reacted: "Dear woman, if you can only see your body as disgraceful and inferior, then why don't you leave this world right now?"

That was just the answer she had been praying for! "Son of the house, if I may, I would do this even today!" she replied.

The merchant said, "Very well then, I shall set you free today." And after he had given the monastery a very generous donation, he brought her to the nuns and had her ordained in the congregation of Devadatta. When she was ordained it was a fulfillment of what she had wanted for a long time.

When it clearly became visible that she was with child, the nuns asked her, "Madam, it appears you are pregnant; what does this mean?"

"Sisters," she replied, "I really did not know this when I was ordained. But my behavior has always been moral."

Then the nuns brought her before Devadatta and asked him, "Master, this lady was ordained after she had persuaded her husband, but now she appears to be pregnant. We do not know for sure if she became pregnant when she was still at home, or after she had been ordained. What are we to do now?"

Devadatta, who in those days was not yet enlightened and did not yet know the values of tolerance, goodwill, or kindness, thought: "What would they think when someone hears that a nun of Devadatta's congregation is with child and Devadatta condones it? It seems fit to me to annul her ordination." So, on impulse and without further inquiry, like sweeping some pebbles from the table, he said, "Go and remove her from our order right now." After these harsh words, the nuns rose, paid their respects, and returned to their quarters.

But the girl said to the nuns, "Sisters, Elder Devadatta is neither the Buddha, nor did he ordain me; my ordination was from the Buddha himself, the greatest man on earth. Do not deny me what I have attained with so much hardship. So come, take me to the Master at Jetavana."

And so the sisters went with her and they traveled over forty-five leagues from Rajagaha to finally reach Jetavana, where they paid homage to the Teacher and told him the whole story.

The Teacher thought, "Although she became pregnant when she still lived at home, there might be a chance that other schools will say that the recluse Gautama accepted someone who had been defrocked by Devadatta[11]. . . . So it seems proper to me to avoid that gossip and come to a judgment on this matter in the presence of the king and his court." And that is what he told the nuns.

The next day, he sent for king Pasenadi the Kosalan and the younger Anathapindika, lady Visakha the great lay disciple, and other well-known heads of families. And in the evening of that day, when the whole congregation was assembled, Gautama requested of elder Upali: "Now, take action to clarify the acts of this young nun in this assembly."

"I shall do so, Reverend Sir," said the elder, and in the congregation, seated before the king, he called Visakha and told her what this was about, after which he placed the matter in her hands: "Go, Visakha, and find out on which day and month it was when the girl was ordained; then judge if it was before or after her ordination that she conceived."

The laywoman agreed and examined the girl, which revealed that she had conceived while she still lived at home. She brought this determination to the elder, who thereupon declared the nun innocent. Thus she was reinstated into the order and before the Master, and together with the nuns she returned to their own monastery.

When her time to give birth came, she had a son, strong in spirit, as she had wished when making a wish at the feet of the Buddha Padumuttara. And one day, when the king was visiting the nuns and heard this child's voice, he asked his servants who this was. When they were informed, they told him, "That young nun gave birth to a boy child, and it is his voice we hear."

The king said, "I would say tending a child in this place is a hindrance to the other nuns; we shall educate him from now on."

So the king had the child brought up by his courtiers, and he was reared as a young noble. On his naming day they called him Kassapa, and later he was known as Kumara-Kassapa. On his seventh birthday he was made a novice with the Teacher; when he was old enough he was fully ordained. As time went by, he became noted among religious preachers for his sparkling eloquence.

Both he and his mother ultimately reached the utmost realization.

৯৯

After the rounds for alms and meals, and after he exhorted his monks, the Teacher retired to his Fragrant Hut.

The monks spent their days in their own quarters, and in the evenings they would gather to sit together in the temple and praise the virtues of the Buddha—for instance, how mother and son had found shelter in him. Then the Master would enter with his Buddha grace and ask, "What were you talking about this time?"

"Reverend Sir, we were talking about your virtues," they would say, and tell him about the day's theme.

On this particular day, the Master said, "Monks, not only now was the Tathâgatha a refuge for these two; he was so in the past as well."

The monks begged the Blessed One to tell them more about this. And the Blessed One made clear what was hidden behind the wheel of rebirth.

A long time ago, when Brahmadatta was reigning in Benares, the Bodhisattva was reborn as a deer. When his mother gave birth to him, he had a golden hue, his eyes were like round jewels, his horns were silver colored, his mouth had the color of the deepest red, his hooves shone like polished lacquer, his tail was like a yak's, and his body was as large as a foal's. He was dwelling in the forest in a herd of five hundred deer and was called Banyan Deer King.

Not very far from there grazed another deer with his herd of five hundred; his name was Branch Deer, and his fur was also of a golden hue.

Those days the king of Benares was fond of hunting deer and had no meal without deer meat. For his daily hunting parties he used to assemble town and countrymen. These men discussed the matter among themselves: "These royal hunting parties are interrupting our work . It would be better if we were to bring deer food and water to his palace park, fix a fence around it, and then drive a lot of deer into his park, close the gate, and then offer this to the king. He would have enough deer for every meal."

And so it happened. When they had brought enough food and water and fixed a fence with a gate around the park, the men from city and country assembled with sticks and other weaponry, and entered the forest to look for deer. They encircled a space of a league, where both deer kings were living with their herds.

When they saw the deer, the men began hitting trees and bushes in order to drive the deer from their shelters, making a great din with their weapons—swords, javelins, and bows. And they drove all the deer into the royal park and shut the gate. Then they went to the king and said: "Majesty, if we have to join you all the time in your deer hunting, we shall not get our work done. So now we have brought the deer to you in this park. From now on you can eat their flesh." And they saluted and left.

The king, after hearing what they said, immediately went to see the deer in his park. And when he saw those two golden deer he resolved that those two were not to be killed. From that day on he sometimes went to the park by himself to shoot a deer and bring it to the palace; sometimes he ordered the game keeper to do so. As soon as the deer saw the bow and arrow, with deadly fear they ran away and after two or three shots they faltered, fainted, and were dead.

Some deer told the Bodhisattva, or in this tale, Banyan Deer King, what was happening. He sent for Branch Deer and said, "Friend, too many deer are being slaughtered; it may be so that they need to die, but they should not be wounded and perish by those arrows. It would be better for the deer to go to an execution block, in turns, so one day the turn falls on my herd, on your herd the next day. Let the deer whose turn it is lie down with his head on the block so this way the deer will not have to suffer." Branch Deer consented, and this was carried out like they planned. The game keeper only had to take the deer and carry it off.

One day, the turn fell on a pregnant doe of Branch's herd. She went to Branch Deer and said, "Master, I am with young. When I have given birth, we can both go instead of me alone today. Please let the turn pass me by!"

He said, "I cannot make others take your turn. You will have to accept your fate. Go now."

Because she could not expect any help from him, she then went to see the Bodhisattva and told him her story. Hearing her words he said, "So be it. Go, and I shall make the turn pass by you."

Then he himself went and lay down with his head on the block. The game keeper saw him there and thought, "Isn't that the deer king who the king said should not be killed? Why is this?" Quickly he went to see the king and told him. The king got on his chariot and went with a great retinue to the park. When he saw the Bodhisattva lying there he said, "Why, friend deer king? Didn't I give you immunity? Why then are you lying there?"

The banyan deer king answered, "Majesty, a doe, heavy with young, came to me and begged me to let her turn fall on another, because she wanted to give birth. What chould I do? I could not possibly send another one in her place, so now I am offering my life and choose the death that belongs to her. So that is why I have lain my head down here on the block."

The king said, "Friend deer king with the golden hue, even among men I have never seen one with such forbearance, good-will, and kindness. This is pleasing me so well. So now I am giving both you and her the freedom to live."

"If two are given immunity and the others not, how can you be the judge of that, O ruler of men?" asked the deer king.

"Also to the rest I shall give immunity and let them live, Master."

"Majesty, if the rest may live, what about the other four-footed creatures?"

"Even to those I shall give their freedom, Master."

"So, Majesty, if the four-footed may live, what then with the bird flocks?"

"To these also I give it, Master."

"Majesty, if the birds are given immunity, what then will happen to the fish dwelling in the water, what will they do?"

"Even the fish may live, Master."

Thus the Bodhisattva had begged the king's privilege for all living animals. He got on his feet and initiated the king into the five precepts,[11] impressed upon him his plights with the grace of a Buddha, saying, "Carry out your duties, your Majesty! Carrying out your duty toward your parents, sons, daughters, town and country folk. Carrying out justice, you will bring welfare to a happy world, and you yourself will go down the happy road to the bright world beyond this one."

He remained for a few days in the park admonishing the king, and then he returned to the forest with his herd.

And the doe gave birth to a fawn, beautiful and bright as a jasmine flower. He liked to play near the branch deer. When his mother saw this she said, "Son, do not go near him anymore; you'd better play near the "banyan." And, admonishing him, she spoke these lines:

> It is the banyan you should seek;
> Better not seek consort with the branch.
> It is better to die near the banyan
> Than be alive with the branch.

From that time on the deer, who after all had won immunity, could eat from the crops as much as they liked. Because the farmers knew about the immunity given by the king, they did not dare to drive them away or hit them. This caused the farmers to assemble in the king's courtyard and tell the king what happened to their crops.

The king said, "With pleasure I gave my blessing to the miraculous banyan deer king; I would rather give up my kingdom than break my word. Go now! Let no one in my kingdom hurt the deer."

The banyan deer king, who heard what was going on, assembled his herd and forbid them henceforth to eat the crops of others. And he let the men know: "From now on the corn growers do not have to make fences to protect their crops."

And never again was a deer seen in the cornfields, because the Bodhisattva had said so. And with this wise admonishing he remained with them all his life, and did many other good deeds.

And the king, too, kept his promises, reigned in wisdom and did not kill another living being for as long as he lived.

☙

The Teacher ended his story saying: "The branch deer is the present Devadatta, his herd is now his congregation of monks, the doe is now Theri, her child is now prince Kassapa, the king is now Ananda, and the banyan deer, that is I."

– 4 –
The Dead Man's Food
«Matakabhatta-jataka»

Flesh should no longer slay flesh
Grief of the soul is the slayer's lot.

This the Master taught while he was living at Jetavana.

In those days it was common pactice, when one's kinsmen died, to have many goats, sheep, and the like, slaughtered as a "food for the dead."

Monks who saw this asked the Teacher, "Reverend Sir, do those traditions serve any purpose?"

The Master replied, "No, brothers, though they think that by killing those animals the deceased are fed, these acts are absolutely uselessr. In times past, the wise were above all that and they warned of the dangers. They made all of Jambudipa[13] abandon these habits. But now they are doing it again, because of their confusion in past lives."

And he told them about the past.

❧

Long ago, when Brahmadatta reigned over Benares, a Brahman,[14] master of the Three Vedas and a leading teacher, wanted to sacrifice a goat to the spirit of the dead, and he told his pupils, "My sons, take this goat to the river, clean it, groom it, hang a garland around its neck, and then bring it back."

So they did and then put it on the riverbank. The goat, aware of its karma (fate) from the past, rejoiced and thought: "Finally, today I am being freed from all this ill!" And she laughed so loud, it sounded like the smashing of a piece of pottery. But immediately afterwards she thought, "When this Brahman has slaughtered me, he will take over all this ill!" So now, feeling pity for him, she started crying out loud.

Then the young Brahmans asked: "Dear goat, first you laugh very loudly, then again you weep very loudly; why is that?"

"Ask me again with my own master present," answered the goat. And they took her to the master and told him. The Teacher then asked the same question. Then the goat told about remembering its past lives: "Brahman, in the past I was a mantra-reciting Brahman just like you. I, too, slaughtered a goat on behalf of the dead, just like you. Because I had killed the goat, I was decapitated in five hundred lives after that, save one. This is the five- hundredth life, which is why I laughed so loudly, thinking 'Finally, this is the last, now I shall be free.' But then again I wept, out of pity for you, because after this life, you are about to live through all those lives as well."

"Do not fear, goat, we shall not kill you," assured the Brahman.

"Brahman, what do you tell me now? Whether you kill me or not, you cannot prevent me from dying today," the goat said.

"Goat, fear not, I shall have you guarded and I shall be with you all day."

"Brahman, your guard will be of no avail, because the evil I did was very strong."

Still they all guarded the goat like she was royalty, and took it with them.

The goat stretched out her neck over a bush growing on a rock, and ate the leaves. At the same moment, lightning struck that very same rock. A splinter coming from the rock exactly hit the goat's neck and cut her head off. The Brahmans and a whole crowd stood around the place were it happened.

Then the Bodhisattva, who had been reborn as the spirit of a tree, saw all those people standing there, and sitting cross-legged in the air, suspended by his special powers as a deva, he thought: "By seeing this happening, those people ought to finally realize the fruit of evil and desist from taking lives."

And he taught them with this verse:

If only men knew and realized
These birth series are fruitless.
Flesh should no longer slay flesh;
Grief of the soul is the slayer's lot.

Thus taught the Great Being the right way, and the people who really listened refrained from taking life. And the Bodhisattva continued dispensing goodness; and the people, working merit, became dwellers of deva city.

– 5 –
Drinking through Cane
«Nala-pana-jataka»

We shall drink the water through a cane;
Thus you certainly shall not devour us.

These lines the Teacher taught while traveling among the Kosalese people and upon their arrival at the village of Nalakapana,[12] where they stayed in the Ketaka forest among the reeds.

The monks, who had taken a bath in the pond, received reed stems, harvested by the novices, in order to make needle cases. They saw that the stems were hollow throughout, and they asked the Teacher how they came to be this way. The Teacher said: "This, brothers, was something I made so, long, long ago." And he recalled the past.

It is said that this forest used to be a dense jungle. The lake housed a water demon who ate everyone who went down to the lake. The Bodhisattva was then living as a monkey king as big as a red deer's fawn, leading a community of over eighty thousand apes dwelling in this jungle. He used to admonish his community: "My loved ones, in this jungle are both poisonous trees and lakes infested with non-human beings. If you think about eating any fruits you have never eaten before, or drinking water you have never drunk before, ask me first."

They were all ears, saying: "Very well, your highness, we shall."

One day, they came to a place where they had not been before. They had been wandering about for most of the day, so they were looking for a place to drink, and when they saw a lake they did not drink but sat still waiting foy the Bodhisattva to come. When he arrived, he asked, "Why, my beloved ones, are you not drinking?"

They replied, "We were waiting for you to come and approve, our lord."

"Well done, my dear ones," said the Bodhisattva, and carefully he scrutinized the lake. He saw all kinds of tracks leading toward it, but none going away. Then he knew, "No doubt this lake is haunted by non-humans. You have done well by not drinking this water."

And the water demon, noting they did not try to come down to the lake, changed himself into a colorful, gruesome being with a blue belly, red hands and feet, and rising out of the water, he said, "What are you waiting for? Come down and drink!"

Thereupon the Bodhisattva asked: "Are you the water demon of this lake?"

"Yes, I am," was his answer.

"And you seize everyone who goes down to the lake?"

"Yes, I seize them all. I never let anyone go who comes down here, not even a little bird. And I shall devour you, too."

The Bodhisattva remained calm and said, "We are definitely not willing to give ourselves to you to eat."

"But you will go down to the lake to drink from the water?" asked the demon.

"Yes, we shall drink from the water, but we shall not be overpowered by you," said the ape king.

"How then will you drink from the water?"

"Well, while you think we must go down there to drink, we shall comfortably remain up here, and all eighty thousand will take a hollow reed-stem and drink from the lake. That way you will not be able to devour us."

When the Teacher had become the very Buddha, he fully understood this matter and uttered this verse:

Since no up-faring track I saw,
But only tracks leading downward,
We shall drink the water through a cane;
Thus you certainly shall not devour us.

After he had addressed the water-demon this way, the Bodhisattva had a reed-stem brought to him and while he turned his mind to the Ten Perfections and performed the Truth Ritual, he blew one time through the reed. This made the reed become quite hollow, without any knot left in it.

Because the power of the Bodhisattva to do good truly reaches far, he was able to perform this deed. From this day on, all reed stems around the lake became hollow, bottom to top.

The Bodhisattva sat down, and took a reed in his hands. And so did the eighty thousand apes sitting around the lake. When the Bodhisattva sucked up the water through his cane, they all joined him in a drink while sitting high and dry on the banks.

And the water demon could not touch anyone of them; so, disillusioned, he descended to his own domain.

Afterwards, the Bodhisattva went back into the jungle with his following.

And the Master recounted the rebirths and assigned the jataka: "The water demon of those days is Devadatta, the eighty thousand apes are now the Buddha community, and the ape king, that was I."

– 6 –
The Antelope
«Kurunga-jataka»

I shall go and get another fruit
For I am not fain to taste thy fruit anymore.

This tale about Devadatta the Master taught while living in the Bamboo Wood.

One day the monks sat assembled in the chapel, chatting in dispraise of Devadatta. They said, "Venerable Devadatta has sent for archers to shoot the Tathâgatha, caused a big rock to smash him, let loose an elephant; he did everything in order to kill Him-of-the-ten-powers."

The Teacher came in, sat down in his seat and asked, "May I ask what you were talking about?" And when they told him, he said, "Brothers, not only nowadays Devadatta has tried to kill me; he sought to do that also in the past, but he never achieve his aim."

And he told about bygone times.

In bygone days, when Brahmadatta was reigning at Benares, the Bodhisattva took birth as an antelope, dwelling in a forest and feeding on all kinds of tree fruits.

One day he was eating from the fruits of a sepanni tree. Now, a deerstalker from the village, who was tracking some deer, had constructed a tree hut so he could watch the deer that were coming to eat from the tree, then outsmart them and sell their meat for his living. So, when he discovered the Bodhisattva's tracks beneath this tree, after an early breakfast he climbed onto the platform and waited with his javelin for the antelope to appear.

The Bodhisattva antelope also had left his lair early that day, thinking, "Today I am going to eat this delicious sepannis." Quietly, he walked toward the tree. But he knew that sometimes there were deer hunters sitting in that tree, so he approached very carefully. At a distance, still unseen, he inspected the scene.

The hunter, who understood that the antelope would not come closer, sat on his platform and threw a few sepannis down in front of the antelope.

The Bodhisattva wondered, "How is it that these fruits are falling just here in front of me? Would there be a hunter up there?"

And looking up, he discovered the hunter. But acting as if he had not seen him, he said, "Dear tree, you used to let your fruit fall straight down from your branches, but today you obviously forgot your tree nature. So now I'd better go get my food from another tree." And he spoke these lines:

> *Known to the antelope it is*
> *What thou, sepanni, art dropping down.*
> *I shall now go and get another fruit*
> *For I am not fain to taste thy fruit anymore.*

Then the hunter threw his javelin from the platform, yelling: "Go! This time I have lost!"

The Bodhisattva turned around and said, "My dear man, it is true that this time you have lost, but the punishment for all your deeds—this you surely did not loose!"

After these words, he bounded away, free to go wherever he wished.

And the hunter, coming down from his lookout, was free to go wherever he wished.

The Teacher ended this jataka with the words: "The deerstalker of those days is Devadatta, and the antelope was just I."

– 7 –
The Bhoja Thoroughbred
«Bhojâjaniya-jataka»

Rider, harness me again!

The Teacher told this tale while living at the Jetavana monastery, about a monk who gave up effort.

He then spoke to that monk and said, "In days of old, monks were working very energetically, even when they could not see where they would end up; just because of their dedication they never gave up." And he recalled the past.

In the past, when Brahmadatta was reigning at Benares, the Bodhisattva was born as a thoroughbred Bhoja horse from Scindh, and he was made king of Benares' state chargers. He was given every kind of decoration. He was fed only three-year-old rice of the finest flavor, served on a precious gold dish, and he stood in a stable with the loveliest perfumes. All around him were crimson curtains; above him a canopy with gold stars, and garlands and floral wreaths hung everywhere, with a perpetual scent of perfumed oil.

The kings of the cities around Benares were always envious of the kingdom of Benares, so one day seven kings dared to surround the city and send a message to the king, demanding: "Your choice: either hand over the kingdom or face us in battle!"

The king assembled his ministers and informed them about

the situation, saying, "Well then, old friends, what do we do now?"

"Sire, you should not go out to fight yet. First send an envoy from the cavalry to either negotiate or fight; if he does not come back, we shall know what to do."

So the king sent for his best rider. "*Tata*, will you be able to give battle to seven kings?" the king asked.

"Sire, if I am allowed to ride the Scindhian Bhoja thoroughbred, I shall fight every king of Jambudipa, let alone those seven," he replied.

"*Tata*, whether you take the Scindhian or some other horse, take what you want and do it!"

"I shall, Sire," said the cavalier, bowing before he left.

Coming down from the palace, he went directly to the stables and had this horse brought out, and completely clad in mail. Then he donned all his own armor, and girded with his sword, he charged at the besiegers. Like a flash of lightning, he dashed through the first entrenchment, taking one king alive, returned to the gates, and handed him over to the guards. Once more he rushed toward the second entrenchment, and the third, and thus taking five kings alive, he broke through the sixth entrenchment. When he had taken the sixth king alive, the thoroughbred was wounded; he had lost a lot of blood and was in great pain. When the cavalier saw the state he was in, he made him lie down at the king's gate, and after he had loosened the mail, he left to arm another horse for the battle.

The Bodhisattva, who lay on his least painful side, opened his eyes and while he followed the rider with his eyes he thought,: "Now he is going to arm another horse, but that one will not be able to break through the seventh and last entrenchment and capture the seventh king. What I accomplished will be in vain; this peerless cavalier will be lost to that army and our king, too, will fall into the enemy's hands. Except for myself, there is no other charger that can do what remains to be done."

So he called back the rider and said, "Good cavalier, no other horse but I will be able to break through the seventh entrenchment and capture this seventh king. I shall not allow the undoing of what I accomplished; so now help me up and arm me once more!" And he spoke these lines:

Though lying on his side and wounded sore by arrow and sword,
This stallion is stronger! Rider, harness me again!

The cavalier helped him get to his feet, bound his wound, fixed his armor, and jumped on his back. Bravely they rode out, broke through the seventh line of defense, took the seventh king alive and handed him over to the king of Benares.

The Bodhisattva was also brought to the palace gates. The king came out to see the stallion. The Great Being said to the king, "Your Majesty, do not slay the seven kings. Make them swear an oath of loyalty and set them free. And let the renown due to me and the brave cavalier be given only to this cavalier. It would not be right to send a warrior, who caught seven kings alive, away empty-handed. Give your rewards, keep your morals, and rule your kingdom with righteousness and justice."

And the king had him taken care of so his wounds could heal quickly; and he gave all honors to the cavalier, made the seven kings take an oath that they would never attack him again and sent them home with their armies. And he reigned with righteousness and justice as long as he lived.

When the Teacher had told this story to the monk who had given up effort, this monk instantly attained the fruits of sainthood. The Teacher, after bringing up this righteous discourse, concluded this Jataka with the words: "The king of those days is Ananda, the cavalier is Sariputta, and the Scindhian Bhoja thoroughbred was just I."

– 8 –
The Mosquito
«Makasa-jataka»

Better a foe who has won some sense...
Than a friend of any sense bereft

This story the Master told in a certain village during his journey among the Magadhese, about villagers who behaved like fools.

They say that the Tathâgatha, after he left Savatthi, took a tour of the kingdom of Magadha, and he arrived at a little hamlet. This village was mainly known for the blind folly of its inhabitants.

One summer day, the men of the hamlet assembled to confer. They said: "Fellow men, when are at work in the forest there are these awful mosquitoes biting us, causing us oftentimes to interrupt our work. Let us take our bows and arrows and other weapons, and declare war upon the mosquitoes. We shall kill them all and cut them to pieces!"

So they entered the forest and in their foolishness, thinking they could hit the mosquitoes, they only hit each other black and blue. Beat-up, they returned to the village, and just dropped down everywhere, at the marketplace and near the gate. Then the Master arrived with his train of monks, begging for alms.

There were some wise men in the hamlet who did not taken part in this senseless mosquito hunt. When they saw the Teacher, they quickly erected a pavilion at the gate and made many offerings; they saluted him and sat down in front of him.

When the Teacher saw all those wounded men lying around he asked, "So many men are hurt; what happened?"

They answered: "Reverend Lord, these men waged war on the mosquitoes in the woods, but only wounded each other instead."

The Master said, "Not only today, but also in the past there were blind fools who thought they could slay mosquitoes."

And the men at his feet begged him to tell the story.

In the past, when Brahmadatta reigned at Benares, the Bodhisattva made his living as a trader. In those days, many woodcraftsmen were living in a border village in the kingdom of Kasi.

One of these men was busy planing a tree, and a mosquito landed exactly on his bald head, which shone like a copper plate. And as if a dart hit him, he instantly got the mosquito's sting in his head.

He said to his son, who sat next to him, "*Tata*, I have been stung by a mosquito; it is like being hit by a dart!"

His son yelled, "*Tata*, hold still; I shall hit it with one blow."

Just at that moment the Bodhisattva, who was shopping, passed by their workshop. The woodcraftsman shouted to his son, "Now, *tata*, hit this mosquito now!"

The son said, "Yes, now I shall kill it, *tata*!" Standing behind his father, he raised a sharp axe, hit hard and . . . broke his father's head in two. The woodcraftsman died on the spot.

When the Bodhisattva saw what happened, he thought, "Better to have a wise foe, because he will not kill, for fear of retribution." And he spoke these lines:

Better a foe who has won some sense,
Than a friend of any sense bereft.
The silly babbler says "I'll kill this gnat!"
And breaks his own father's crown.

After he had said this, the Bodhisattva arose and went on his way. And the kinsmen of the woodcraftsman carried off his body.

The son, however, had learned his lesson. He followed the

Master on his tour, did many penances and ultimately was accepted as a monk.

The Teacher concluded this Jataka with the words: "And the wise trader who spoke and went on, that was just I."

– 9 –
The Neglected Park
«Arama-dusaka-tataka»

When for welfare it is not fit,
Work for welfare brings no pleasure.

This is a story about a spoiled garden, the Master related in a little village in the region of Kosala.

The story goes that the Master, traveling among the Kosalese, reached this village. There, a landowner invited the Tathâgatha to take a rest in his garden, and after he had served all the guests he said, "Reverend sirs, why don't you take a walk in my garden?"

The monks stood up and walked with the groundskeeper through the park. Seeing an unusual, barren space, they asked him, "In this garden there is dense vegetation everywhere, except on this spot. Here grows neither tree nor bush. Why so?"

And the man answered, "Reverend sirs, when this park came to be, there was a village boy who watered all these plants. From this spot he removed all the young trees. He only watered the large trees. He would uproot all the young shoots from the ground and check to see if the roots were big enough. So all the young trees died, and that is why this spot became bare."

After the monks told this strange story to the Teacher, he said, "Monks, this village lad was not only in this time a garden spoiler; he did the same in the past." And he told the tale about this boy's past life.

ॐ

In times past, when Brahmadatta reigned at Benares, in the city they organized a big festival. When the sound of the drums was heard, everyone knew they could start celebrating.

In those days there were many monkeys in the king's garden. The groundskeeper thought with envy, "Now the festival begins in the city, while I am stuck here. I have an idea: if I ask the monkeys to water the trees for me, I can still join the party." And he went to the senior monkey and asked him, "Greetings, senior monkey, this garden is of great use for you monkeys; you eat its flowers, fruits, and young shoots. Today there is a big festival in the city and I would love to be there. Would you be so kind and water the young plants until I return?"

And the monkey said, "All right, I shall water them."

"Well then, take good care," said the gardener, and after he had given some buckets and watering skins to the monkeys, he left for the city and mingled with the reveling crowd.

The monkeys then began watering the young trees. The elder monkey told them, "You will have to be more economical with the water. When you are watering the young shoots, always pull them out first to see if their roots are long enough. If so, give them water; if not give little water. Otherwise we shall not have enough for the whole garden." And so they did.

At that moment, a wise man passed by who saw the monkeys doing this in the king's garden, and he said, "What on earth are you doing, monkeys! Why do you uproot every young shoot and only water according to the size of the root?"

They replied: "This is what our head man told us to do."

When the wise man heard this he shook his head and thought: "Alas! This way the fools, saying they will make it better, actually make it worse!" And he spoke these lines:

When for welfare it is not fit,
Work for welfare brings no pleasure.
The stupid man undoes the weal,
As does the monkey in this park.

With this saying, the wise man reprimanded the monkeys and then left the garden with his following. And the monkeys took the lesson to heart, and undid what they had done.

The Teacher then concluded this jataka, saying, "The senior monkey is now the neglectful village boy, but the wise man, that was just I."

– 10 –
The Great King Silavant
«Mahasilava-jataka»

When I look at the other, I see myself:
As I wish, so I become.

This the Teacher told while living at the Jetavana monastery, about a monk who had relinquished effort.

He asked this monk, "Why did you, brother, in such a far-reaching religion as ours, already give up effort? In earlier days, wise men were able to keep their integrity—even when they lost their kingdoms, even if they were struck down—by standing on their own effort." And he told this tale.

In the past, the Bodhisattva, a gifted son, succeeded his father to become the king named Silavant ("Moral"), and reigned at Benares as a righteous and equitable monarch.

At each of the four city gates, and in the city center and at the palace gates, he erected a hall where people could bring gifts for poor folk and wayfarers. He protected the moral code, kept holy days and always showed patience, goodwill, and kindness; he cherished all creatures like a father cherishes his child on his lap.

One of his courtiers had behaved badly in the harem, and when the king was informed about this, he told him, "You fool, what you did was shameful; you do not deserve to live in my land. Take what is yours, including your family, and go live somewhere else."

And so this man left the Kasi kingdom for Kosala and offered himself into the service of the court there, where he earned the king's confidence.

One day it came to the Kosala king's attention that the king of Benares was exceedingly kind-hearted, and the kingdom was like an untouched honeycomb, needing scarcely an army to conquer it.

But the Benares kingdom was large, and the Kosala king was afraid the man might be a spy in the service of Benares. But the man advised him anyway to initially send a group of raiding warriors, as a test, into the land of Kasi. He said that if these were to be caught and led before the king, they would be released, and even would be given gifts. Indeed, this happened twice, and the third time the robbers even entered Benares city.

Then the Kosala king said that the Benares king was indeed much too righteous, so he decided to occupy the kingdom.

The thousand extremely brave soldiers from Benares could not persuade their king to let them repel the invaders. "*Tatas*," he said, "no injury to anyone should be committed in my name. If this king decides to seize our kingdom, let him do so. Do not intervene." And none of their plea ding could change his mind.

When the Kosala king entered the city on horseback, he did not meet any resistance, and the doors to the royal dwellings stood wide open. Arriving at the great terrace where the impeccable Benares king sat with his ministers, he gave orders to seize them, bind them, and carry them off to the graveyard, where they were to bury them up to their throats and leave them to the mercy of the jackals.

But even then, king Silavant did not resist the arrest, nor disobeyed any of the Kosala king's orders.

So there they were, trapped in the solidly tamped soil, abandoned—and even the Benares king exhorted his men not to have vindictive feelings toward the bandit king, but rather practice goodwill.

Then the jackals came, in the middle of the night. The king and his men yelled themselves hoarse, and the beasts at first dashed away, but slowly, their hunger got the better of them, and they came close to seizing their prey. The leader of the jackals had it in for the king's head.

The king, who was a skillful strategist, saw the jackal coming and bent his head backward, showing it his throat. When the jackal came very close, it was the king who had the jackal by the throat, gripping it tight as a vise. The jackal, in mortal fear, raised a mighty howl, so the rest of the pack fled frantically, tails between their legs. But the jackal that was trapped between the king's teeth wrestled violently to escape, loosening the earth around the king's head with its feet. When the king saw that the earth around him was loose, he let go of the jackal. With an elephant's strength, he wrung his arms loose and pulled himself out of the hole, and then drew the others from their imprisonment.

There were two *yakkhas*[16] who both owned part of the graveyard, and someone had brought a corpse and laid it exactly on the boundary of the two sectors. So they were quarreling about who had rights to the body.

When the king walked by they said, "This king Silavant is righteous, he will determine justice for us." When they asked the king, he said, "Good *yakkhas*, I shall, but as you see, I am very dirty, so first I need to take a bath." The *yakkhas* immediately used their magic to create a bath for the king; they brought him clean garments from the bandit king, perfume, and flowers. Was there anything else they could do for him? Yes, he would like something to eat. And they brought him all kinds of food, drinking water, and water for washing hands and mouth, and betel leaves to chew. Something else? Yes, he wanted the state sword, lying beside the bandit king's head.

When he obtained the sword, the king split the corpse into two halves, and gave half to each *yakkha*.

Then they ate together and were satisfied. Now was there anything else they could do for the king?

"Yes, bring me to the sleeping quarters of the bandit king and take my men to his home," answered the king.

When he arrived at the house, the Benares king went straight to the bedroom where the bandit king was sleeping in his own bed, and hit him on the stomach with the flat of his sword. He awoke with a shock, saw in the lamplight who stood at his bedside, and when he came to his senses he asked, perplexed, "Majesty, how is it possible that you, at this hour of the night, with guards in front and around the house, gates closed, still got in, fully adorned and armed with my own sword?"

The king told him the whole story. When he had heard this, the bandit king was totally dumbstruck. After a while he could only mumble, "Majesty, I did not know anything about your good deeds, and yet the fierce, rough *yakkhas*, eaters of their enemy's flesh, knew you well. From now on, Lord of men, I shall never ever harm someone as good as you."

And he swore an oath on his sword and got the king's forgiveness. He offered the king his own royal bed to sleep on, while he slept on a small one.

At sunrise the bandit king had the beat of the tom-tom call into assembly the entire army and the populace, and addressed them publicly about the virtues of the king. He also publicly apologized and returned the kingdom to them. To the king he said, "The threat by bandits to your kingdom is my karma. But from this moment I shall keep watch and guard you against all danger."

He also gave orders to punish the man who had betrayed the good king.

Silavant, the great king, back on his throne in his palace, thought, "Our sitting here again, with the lives of my subjects and ministers saved, would not have been so if I had made no effort. By the strength of my effort I avoided this doom and gave everyone a new life. Truly, without the use of the sword, man should keep on trying his best; only then will his work bear fruit." And he was inspired to utter these lines:

Man should never lose hope; the wise should not falter.
When I look at the other, I see myself:
As I wish, so I become.

And working merit unceasingly, Silavant, the Bodhisattva, remained loyal to his heart in words and deeds.

Upon hearing this story, the hopeless monk regained his feeling of self-esteem, and the Master concluded this jataka saying, "This mischievous courtier of the king in those days is Devadatta, the ministers are now my followers, and king Silavant, that was I."

– 11 –
The Gold Nugget
«Kancanakkhanda-jataka»

He of gladsome heart . . . in due course may succeed
In bringing ev'ry hindrance to an end.

When living at Savatthi, the Teacher told this story about a monk.

Once upon a time, a man of the Savatthi family, after having heard the righteous teachings of the Master, gave his heart to the religion of the Jewels,[17] and withdrew from the world.

Then he received from his teacher and his tutor the following moral code:

"Revered One, the moral code has many faces, up to ten kinds; there is a minor code, a middle code, and the highest code.[18] We are giving you now the moral code of restraint of sense and restraint by purity in subsistence."

The man was thinking, "This moral code really is too vast. If I have to keep up with all these rules, I shall not make it. What is the use of me withdrawing from the world and then not being able to live up to those rules? I shall become a layman again, and then will do good works and support a wife and family."

With this resolve, he went to the other monks and said, "Reverend brothers, I shall not be able to keep the moral code, so I must be honest with myself. What is the use of leaving the world like that? I shall return to the ordinary world again. Now will you please take my bowl and robe?"

"So be it," they answered. "Now leave, after saluting the Ten-powered One." And they brought him before the Teacher in the temple. When the Master saw them he asked, "Why, brothers, do you bring a monk who has resigned?"

"Reverend Sir, this monk is returning his bowl and robe and says he will not be able to keep the moral code; that is why we are bringing him here."

The Teacher said, "But brothers, why did you oblige him with so many rules? As much as he can handle, that should be enough for him. So this is not the way it should go. I know a way."

And he asked the monk, "Well then, brother, such a lot of rules you cannot keep. Do you think you can handle just three?"

"Sure I can, Reverend Sir," said the monk.

"All right, now direct your attention to ward the three 'gates': the 'gate' of the act, the 'gate' of the word and the 'gate' of the thought. Do no evil deeds, utter no evil words, keep no evil thoughts. Go now, do not turn back to the lower life; just act according these three rules."

Thereupon the monk, glad at heart, said, "Very well, Reverend Sir, I shall keep these three precepts." He saluted the Master and left the room with his teacher and tutor.

And while he did his best to remain pure in deeds, words, and thoughts, he came to this awareness: "Although the moral code was explained to me by my teacher and tutor, they were not able to clarify them, because they were not ready themselves. But the Enlightened One, because of his enlightened state of Being, and because he himself is a living example of the state, could make me grasp the moral code, be it just three 'gates'! Ah! Such a solid bedrock the Teacher has made for me!"

The insight unfurled quickly within him, because in only a matter of days he attained the state of sanctity.

When the monks, assembled in the temple, learned about this, they praised the virtues of the Buddha. The Teacher came in and heard them talking.

"Brothers," he said, "No matter how heavy a burden may be, when analyzed bit by bit, it becomes very easy to bear. Wise men in times past, when they found a big nugget of gold they could not lift, found that they could carry it easily when it was divided among them."

And he recalled the past.

In days past, when Brahmadatta was king of Benares, the Bodhisattva was born in a hamlet as a son of a farmer.

One day, he was plowing a field, beneath which another hamlet from bygone times lay buried. In those times, a very wealthy merchant had hoarded a gold nugget as thick as a man's thigh and four cubits in length. On this nugget the Bodhisattva's plow got caught and stood fast. At first he thought it was an outgrowth of a big root, but when he cleared away the soil and discovered what it was, he covered it up again and just continued plowing that day.

At sunset, he put aside the plow and yoke, and thought, "Now I shall dig up this gold nugget." But of course he was not able to lift it on his own. What now? He sat down and thought, "So much I shall use for food, so much I shall put aside for savings, so much I shall use to trade, and another part is for working merit," and this way he already divided the nugget in his mind.

To him, dividing it like this in his mind, the gold nugget seemed to become very light. He could now lift it, brought it home, divided it into four parts, and lived the rest of his days in peace and did many good deeds.[19]

The Exalted One, being the Very Enlightened, revealed this lesson and spoke these lines:

> *He of gladsome heart,*
> *The man who's joyful in mind,—*
> *He makes goodness come to be,*
> *To win the goal he seeks;*

He in due course may succeed
In bringing ev'ry hindrance to an end.

Thus the Master completed the lesson with the words: "That man who found the gold nugget, that was I."

– 12 –
The Clever Monkey
«Vanarinda-jataka»

He surely will outrun his foe

While he was living in the Bamboo Woods, the teacher gave this lesson about Devadatta's efforts to kill him.

"Not only now, brothers," he said, "does he do so; he tried many times in the past, but he was not able to destroy me."

And he recalled the past.

In days of yore, when Brahmadatta reigned at Benares, the Bodhisattva, reborn in the world of monkeys, had grown to be as big as a colt and strong as an elephant, and was living on the riverbank. In the middle of the stream was a small island on which many fruit trees were growing: mangoes, breadfruit, and bananas.

The Bodhisattva would leap from his side of the river to a flat rock lying midway between his bank and the islet, and then take another leap to get to those sweet, delicious fruits. He would eat his fill, and by evening he would leap back to the riverbank. Each day this scene repeated itself; this was his way of keeping himself alive.

At the time, a crocodile and his consort also had a domain in this river. And the wife, seeing the Bodhisattva time and again leap over them, lusted after him a bit, and she told her mate of her craving. The crocodile said, "Very well, I shall get this appetizing ape heart for you." He thought, "Today, when he returns from the island, I shall catch him." And he lay down on the flat rock in the river, waiting for the right moment. . ...

The Bodhisattva, as usual, had spent his day on the islet, and in the evening he stood there, looking at this flat rock. He wondered, "Why does this rock look higher than usual?" Because he used to determine the height of the water and the rock in order to calculate his leap, it occurred to him: "Today there is neither fall nor rise in the height of the water, yet the rock lies higher in the river. I wonder if it is that crocodile lying in wait for me. I shall first test him."

And standing there at the edge of the islet, he addressed the rock, "Master rock!"

He called three times, but because no answer came, he called louder: "Rock!!" The rock did not respond. Then the monkey said, "Why, master rock, do you not answer me today?"

The crocodile thought, "Well, well, this rock must be talking to him on other days; so now I shall ease his mind and answer." And he said, "What is the matter, master monkey?"

The monkey asked, "Who are you?"

The crocodile responded, "I am a crocodile rock," thus giving himself away.

"Why are you lying there?" the monkey asked.

"Hoping to catch your heart's flesh," said the crocodile.

The Bodhisattva thought, "So that is no way to go today; I shall have to find another way around this crocodile." And he told him, "Good sir crocodile, I shall give myself up to you. Open your mouth and catch me as I come."

Now it is a fact that when crocodiles open their mouths, they have to shut their eyes. Always. So now this crocodile, who did not see through the trick, lay there with his mouth wide open and his eyes shut. Then the Bodhisattva leapt from the island on top of the crocodile's head, and thence, with a giant jump, fast as lightning, leapt again to the safe riverbank.

When the crocodile realized what had happened, he thought, "What a marvel this monkey has done!" He said, "Master monkey, someone in this world who has four qualities, overcomes any enemy; you have all four of these, I reckon." And in recognition he spoke these lines:

> He who has these four, lord monkey, as you have—
> Truth, righteousness, resolve, and surrender—
> He surely will outrun his foe."

After this homage to the Bodhisattva, the crocodile returned to his own place.

And the Master resolved this jataka with the words: "Devadatta was the crocodile of those days; the young Brahminee Chincha was his consort , and the monkey lord was just I."

– 13 –
A Woman's Secrets
«Durajana-jataka»

Of women hard the nature it is to fathom
As is the way of a fish in deep waters

This is a story about a lay disciple that the Teacher told while staying at Jetavana.

This disciple of Savatthi had been initiated in the three Gems and the five Precepts (*Ratana-sasana*), devoted to Buddha, *Dhamma*, and *Sangha*. He had a wife who was wicked and immoral. One day she would be the evil woman, acting like a cheap harlot, the next day she was acting like a mistress, fierce and abusive. The husband could not understand her character anymore. And because he was worrying about this, he had stopped waiting on the Buddha.

But one day he did go, taking flowers and perfumes, and after he had bowed to him and taken his seat, the Master asked him, "Why have you not been to visit us lately, brother?"

And he said, "It is my lady, Reverend Sir; one day she behaves like a cheap harlot, the next day as a fierce mistress; I just cannot understand this anymore. Because I have been worrying about this, I could not come to wait on the Buddha."

When the Teacher heard this, he said: "Brother layman, the character of a woman is hard to fathom—so did wise men of the past know even then. One can hardly differentiate, because there is often a confusion from past lives."

And he recalled the past.

ॐ

A long time ago, when Brahmadatta reigned at Benares, the Bodhisattva, having become a world teacher, was instructing five hundred young Brahmans in science.

Among them was a young man from abroad, who fell in love with a woman and, when she became his wife, lived with her in the city of Benares. During this time he absented himself for three terms. The woman whom he married was immoral and disrespectful. One day she behaved like a bad slave and the next day like a proud, humiliating mistress. He could not fathom her nature and she caused him to be worried and confused, so he forgot to visit and serve his Teacher.

When a week had passed, he finally went again, and the Teacher asked, "Why were you absent for a week?"

"Master," he replied, "One day my wife is praying and begging for me like a slave, and the next day she is as obstinate, proud, and patronizing as a mistress. I cannot understand her anymore, and because of this I was too worried to come to you."

The Teacher said, "It is just the way of some women that, when their behavior has been compliant to their husbands, while they have nothing to hide, they behave proudly and unmanageable, and put on airs toward their husbands. This does not excuse or explain their behavior away. Indeed, their characters are hard to fathom. The best is to observe the golden mean, between desiring and not desiring."

And as admonition he spoke these lines:

Do not be glad thinking "She is fain for me!"
Do not be sad thinking: "She is not fain."
Of women hard the nature it is to fathom,
As is the way of a fish in deep waters.

Because of this lesson, the pupil's attitude went toward the golden mean, and he did not allow himself to be carried away by emotion. And his wife thought, "The Teacher knows now of my capricious behavior," so from that moment on she controlled herself.

And so it happened the same way with the layman's wife. He and his wife lived more harmoniously and respectfully toward each other afterwards.

And the Teacher concluded this jataka with these words: "The couple of those days are the couple of today; and the teacher was just I."

– 14 –
Attraction and Affection
«Saketa-jataka»

The man who makes his mind his home. . .
Though he may be a stranger in a strange land
Willingly he feels trust at once.

This jataka, about a Brahman, the Teacher related while staying in the Anjana forest near Saketa.

When the Blessed One was entering Saketa, followed by a long line of monks, an old Brahman from Saketa was just leaving the city. When he saw the Ten-Powered One, he fell on his knees at the Master's feet, grabbed His legs and said, "Dear boy, should not parents in their old age be cherished by their children? Why didn't you show yourself to us for so long, son? Now that I have seen you here, come and see your mother." And he took the Master to his home. In front of his house, the Teacher sat down on the prepared seat, surrounded by his monks. And the Brahman's wife came out and also fell at the Teacher's feet, lamenting, "My darling, where have you been for so long? Should parents when they are old not be ministered too?" And she had the other sons and daughters greet him, too, with the words, "Come on, salute your brother!"

And both parents happily and cordially shared their meal. After they ate, the Master told them about the tenet of old age. At the end, both were established in the stage of Non-returnee's Fruition;[20] afterwards the Master, rising from his seat, went back to the Anjana forest.

The Brahmans sat in their temple and started the talk: "Every Brahman knows that the Thatâgatha's father is Suddhodana and his mother Maya. Still, although he knew this, both this man and his wife called him 'our son,' and the Master let it all happen. What could be the reason?"

The Master overheard their talk and said, "Brothers, both of them spoke of me as their own son," and he recalled the past.

That old Brahman, brothers has been my father for five hundred births in succession; for five hundred births before that he was my uncle; for five hundred births before that he was my grandfather. Also this Brahminee was for five hundred births in immediate succession my mother; for five hundred births before that she was my aunt; for five hundred births before that she was my grandmother. Thus, for fifteen hundred lives I grew up in the hands of this Brahman and Brahminee. In all those lives my enlightened being grew."

And he recited these lines:

> *The man who makes his mind his home*
> *And in whose heart he finds rest—*
> *Though he may be a stranger in a strange land,*
> *Willingly he feels trust at once.*

When the Tahtâgatha was about to leave for the *vihara*,[20] another monk asked, "This attraction, Blessed Lord, what was the cause of this affection?"

> *What, Blessed Lord, may be the cause as hown here—*
> *That for some men the heart is wholly quenched;*
> *For some, mind rests in its pleasant charm?*

Then the Master clarified the cause of attraction:

> *By mutual company in past lives,*
> *Or by benevolence shown in this life,*
> *Thus may affection and love spread*
> *Like the lotus blooms in the water.*

This was the lesson in this jataka, and the Teacher closed with the words: "The Brahman and his wife were those two, and the son was just I."

– 15 –
The Gate to Happiness
«Atthassa dvara-jataka»

. . . These are the six gates
That open to happiness, equaling growth.

This short story the Teacher told when he was living at the Jeta-vana monastery. It is about a son who was doing works of mercy.

In Savatthi there once lived a wealthy, prominent merchant's son who at only seven years old appeared to be wise and generous. One day he went to his father and asked him the meaning of the "gate to happiness." The father did not know the answer and thought, "This is a very subtle question; except for the all-knowing Buddha there is no one, high or low, who can answer it."

So he had his son take garlands and sweet perfumes, and he brought him to Jetavana. He greeted the Master with the offer-ings, sat beside him, and said, "Reverend Sir, this boy is at his young age already wise and generous. He asked me about the 'gate to happiness.' I cannot answer this question, that is why I came to you. It would be well if the Blessed One would explain this."

The Master said, "In bygone days, layman, I was asked the very same question by this youth and we have been talking about it. Then he knew, but because of being born in another life he can-not remember this now."

When the father asked him to tell more about this, the Master recalled the past.

๙

"In past times, when Brahmadatta reigned at Benares, the Bodhisattva was a very wealthy leading merchant. When his son asked him the same as your son has asked you now, the father spoke these lines":

Let him seek good health,
The moral code, deference to elders
Learning righteousness, living in good harmony,
And non-grasping: these are the six gates
That open to happiness, equaling growth.

Thus said the Bodhisattva to his son about the gates to happiness. And from that day he persevered in these six qualities. And the Bodhisattva kept on doing good works, according to his holiness.

The Master concluded this jataka saying, "The son of the past is the present son, and the merchant was just I."

– 16 –
The Lesson the King Learned
«Rajôvada-jataka»

By equanimity he conquers anger, with good he conquers bad. . .

At the Jetavana monastery the Teacher taught this jataka about a king's lesson.

On a certain day, the king of Kosala had administered justice in a case upon which it had been very difficult to pass judgment. After he had his meal, he mounted his decorated chariot and drove all the way up to the Jetavana monastery to see the Teacher. After greeting Him by touching His feet, the king sat down next to Him.

The Teacher asked him, "Well, Your Majesty, why did you come all the way up here at this hour of the day?"

"Reverend Sir, I was not able to come sooner because I had to pass judgment on a very difficult case; afterwards I ate, cleansed myself, and now I have come to wait on you."

The Teacher said, "Your majesty, it is a good thing to judge in court justly and honestly. Isn't it wonderful that those who wish to be spoken to by someone like me should judge a case rightly and justly? Likewise it is wonderful that kings of the past, who did not have the opportunity to listen to the wise, still were able to administer justice in court in a just and honest way. It was their way up to the Bright World."

The king asked him to tell more about this, and the Teacher began:

႙

In the early days, when Brahmadatta still reigned at Benares, the Bodhisattva was reborn to his first wife. On the naming day they gave him the same name as his father's, Brahmadatta.

When he reached sixteen years old, he went to Takkasila and acquired experience and expertise in all kinds of art.

When his father died, he ascended to the throne and ruled rightly, administering justice without prejudice or favoritism. Because of his example, his ministers were also righteous in their judgments; there was no occurrence of fraud. And because there were no more cases of fraud, it was also the end of excessive litigation at the king's court. Although the ministers were present all day, no one came for their counsel, so they eventually went home. The law courts became a negligible necessity.

The Bodhisattva thought, "Because I am reigning righteously, no one is coming to the court anymore; the pressure has gone and the law courts are not in use. Now it is time to do some self-examination. Should I discover any faults or shortcomings, I can recondition myself so I shall progress in virtues."

When he inquired here and there whether somebone could say if he had some faults or shortcomings, no one from his court came forward; everywhere he was only praised for his virtues.

The king thought, "Perhaps they just fear the consequences of telling me," so he inquired outside his court. When he found no one there, either, who could tell him, he asked within the city, then outside, at the four gates, and in the suburbs beyond the gates. And invariably he got the same answers about his good characteristics and deeds, but not about his faults.

"I shall inquire in the countryside," he thought next, and temporarily handed over the kingdom to his ministers. He took his chariot with just the driver, and left the city anonymously.

Everywhere in the country he inquired, even in the borderlands. Even there he could hear not a single word that did not speak of his merits, so he decided to return to the city, taking the main road.

At the same time Mallika, king of Kosala, who was also righteous, had similar thoughts and became a seeker of his shortcomings as well. He also had found no one to reveal them among those within the precincts and the rest; only his virtues were praised. He also had extended his search to the countryside and came to the same borderlands where the Bodhisattva was. And both kings met exactly at a narrow pass between the rocks; there was no room for the two chariots to pass.

Then king Mallika's charioteer told the Benares king's charioteer, "Clear this way for the king's chariot!"

The other answered, "My good man, make your chariot give way; in this chariot is seated the great lord of the kingdom of Benares, king Brahmadatta!"

The other charioteer reacted similarly: "My good charioteer, do you know that in this chariot is seated the lord of the kingdom of Kosala, king Mallika? Now make room for our king, clear the way!"

Brahmadatta's charioteer thought: "So there is indeed another king here. What next? . . . I have an idea! I should ask about his age; the chariot of the younger king ought to make way for the elder."

So he asked the other charioteer how old King Mallika was. When it became clear that both kings were of the exact same age, next he asked about the size of his kingdom, his power. Wealth, fame, caste, clan, family—and soon it was discovered that both rulers had a kingdom of three hundred leagues and were equal in power, wealth, fame, caste, clan and family. . . Next, he thought: "I shall make way for the one who is the most moral in his acts." And he asked, "What about your king's moral conduct?"

And the other enlarged upon his king's moral behavior, setting forth his fault as virtue:

Hard to the hard throws Mallika, and soft to the soft,
Good by the good he conquers, bad by bad:
Such is this king! And now, driver, out of the way!

Then Brahmadatta's charioteer reacted: "Hear what you are saying, good man! Did speak of your king's virtues?"

"Yes," was his answer.

"If these are his virtues, what about his faults then? Listen," the Benares charioteer said. And he attributed these lines to his king:

> *By equanimity he conquers anger, with good he conquers bad;*
> *He will conquer meanness with a gift;*
> *With the truth he responds to those who speak false.*
> *Such is this king! Now driver, out of our way!*

After those wise words, king Mallika and his driver got down from their chariot, unharnessed the horses, pushed the chariot aside, and gave way for the king of Benares.

King Brahmadatta then exhorted king Mallika, saying, "Try to carry out what my charioteer just described." And they returned to Benares.

And the Benares king lived in peace and did good deeds until the end of his life, and then ascended into the Bright World.

King Mallika took the lesson to heart, inquired further in the country, and after unsuccessfully finding any fault, he returned to his own city, working merit in giving and the like, and at the end of his life he, too, ascended into the Bright World.

The Teacher told this story as a lesson for the king, and concluded the Jataka saying, "King Mallika;s charioteer is now Moggallana, king Mallika is now Ananda, the Benares charioteer is now Sariputta, and the Benares king, that was I."

– 17 –
The Man-Eating Yakkha
«Gagga-jataka»

Poison be the goblin's food!
May you live a hundred summers yet!

This tale about a sneeze (yes, a sneeze!) was told by the Teacher when he was living at the Royal Park, built by king Pasenadi.

One day, namely, when the Teacher sat in the midst of the four-fold congregation of monks in the park and was teaching the Way, he sneezed. The monks cheered loudly: "Your health, Blessed One! May the well-farer live!" and made a lot of noise, disturbing the entire religious conversation.

Then the Blessed One asked the monks, "Is it supposed, when one sneezes, and the other says 'May you live,' that one has a choice whether one may live or die?"

"Of course that is not so, Reverend Sir," they said.

"You should not say that anymore, brothers, with every sneeze. Who does so, acts amiss."

In those days, however, it was customary to say, when a monk sneezed: "May you live, reverend sir!" But now the monks were confused and hesitated about how to react. Some even were offended and said: "How is it that the Sakya recluses will not respond from now on?"

When this came to the attention of the Blessed One, he responded smilingly, "Men of the world, brothers, are given to the wish cult. But I gladly grant you, when it is said: 'May you live, reverend sir,' to say: 'And may you live long!'"

And they asked him, "Reverend Sir, when was it that this wish cult first arose?"

"Brothers," he said, "that happened a very long time ago." And he told about those days.

ॐ

Long ago, when Brahmadatta was reigning at Benares, the Bodhisattva was reborn in the Kasi kingdom, in a Brahman family. His father's calling was as general trader. When the boy was about sixteen, his father entrusted him with a consignment of jewelry, and together they traveled to villages and cities. After a long day on the road they finally reached Benares.

Because they did not know where to stay the night, they had a meal prepared at the gatekeeper's house and asked, "Do you know a lodging place for people like us, arriving at such a late hour?"

They were told, "Outside the gates there is a building, but it is haunted by a *yakkha*; but if that does not bother you, you may stay the night there."

The Bodhisattva said, "Come on, *tata*, let us go; we shall not be frightened by a *yakkha*. I shall tame him and get rid of him." And together they went there.

There in the house this *yakkha* had taken up residence, after serving Vessavana for twelve years. Whenever men entered the house and sneezed, he ate them all, save those who said: "May you live!" or "Same to you!" He was living in the attic of the building.

When the Bodhisattva and his father arrived, he thought, "I shall make the Bodhisattva sneeze." And he sprinkled some fine powder that would sneak into the nose, so the people below would sneeze.

But the Bodhisattva did not say: "May you live!"

As a result, the *yakkha* came down from the ridgepole to eat him alive. The Bodhisattva saw him coming and thought, "That is he who caused me and my father to sneeze. It is that man-eating

yakkha who eats everyone who does not answer: 'May you live!'"
To his father he said out loud, so the *yakkha* could hear:

May you live a hundred, Gagga, and then a twenty!
No goblin will eat you! May you live a hundred summers yet!

When the *yakkha* heard this, he thought, "Too bad, I cannot eat this boy because he said the words, but I shall eat the father!" The father saw him coming and thought, "This will be the cannibal *yakkha* who eats everyone who does not say: 'May you live!'" And to his son he said:

May you, too, live a hundred years and another twenty!
Poison be the goblin's food! May you live a hundred summers yet!

Then the *yakkha* gave up and withdrew to his ridgepole.
A little later, the Bodhisattva asked him: "Dear *yakkha*, why is it that you eat people who enter this place?"
"Because that is what Vessavana gave me permission to do, after twelve years of loyal service," he said.
"But were you allowed to eat everyone?" asked the Bodhisattva.
"Everyone but those who says this wish after someone sneezes," was the answer.
"*Yakkha*, in the past you have done those same nasty things, so now you are reborn as this harsh, cruel creature, only hurting others. Now again you are doing the same sort of things and this way you are only imprisoned in the dark, from one life to the next. Give it up now; give up taking life for pleasure forever."
Then the Bodhisattva tamed the creature and he taught him the five *silas*,[22] and then made him a sort of errand boy.
The next morning, people passing by heard what happened to the *yakkha* that night and they told the king. The king sent for the Bodhisattva and placed him in charge of his guilds, and he also paid much honor to his father. And the *yakkha* he made a tax gatherer!
The king was inspired by the Bodhisattva, did many good

works, and at the end of his life he went to fill a place in the Bright World.

And the Teacher concluded this jataka with the words, "The king of those days is Ananda, the father is Kassapa, and the son—you might have guessed—was just I."

– 18 –
The Vulture
«Gijjha-jataka»

"When the other-becoming is at hand,
Even a man dos not heed this inevitable trap...

This tale, about a monk who supported his mother, was narrated by the Teacher while living at the Jetavana monastery.

The Master asked this monk, "Is it true, brother, that you are supporting someone in the outside world?"

When he confirmed this, he was asked, "But what are they to you?"

He replied, "They are my parents, reverend sir," which made the Master nod his head in approval: "Very good, well done."

And he admonished the other monks: "Brothers, do not be vexed with this monk. Wise men of old, by their own virtue, have rendered service even to those not related to them, but this monk takes on the charge of his own parents."

And he told about past times:

Long, long ago, when Brahmadatta was king of Benares, the Bodhisattva was born as a vulture, and he took care of his parents.

One day a mighty snowstorm befell them. The vultures could not withstand this tempest, so, in peril from cold, they quickly flew to Benares where they perched near a city wall.

A prominent merchant from Benares, who was just coming out of the city to take a bath in the river, saw these weary vultures and took them to a dry place. He had a fire lit, sent someone to get cattle flesh from the charnel yard, and set a guard to watch over the birds.

When the storm subsided, the birds, by then recuperated, went back to the hills. Assembled there, they considered: "This Benares trader has altruistically aided us, and as a thank you we shall help him in return. Therefore, if one of us should see a cloth or ornament, he should pick it up and drop it in the merchant's courtyard."

From that day on, the vultures, whenever they saw clothing and ornaments hanging outside, they picked these up like a hawk seizes his prey, and dropped their booty in the open court-yard of the merchant's house.

When this merchant understood what they were doing, he had each piece put away properly.

Then the people told the king: "Vultures are plundering the whole city!"

The king said, "Try to catch one of them, then I shall see to it that they return everything."

And he had traps and nets laid here and there, so very soon the vulture that supported his parents was caught in a trap. He was taken directly to the king.

The merchant, who was just on his way to visit the king, saw that the men were carrying this captured vulture, and he said, "Do not hurt the vulture!" and he went along with them.

When they had brought the bird before the king, the king asked the vulture, "Is it your folk who plunder the city, taking clothes and everything?"

"Yes, Sire, it is," said the vulture.

"To whom are you taking your booty?" asked the king.

"To the leading merchant of Benares, majesty, this man stand-ing here," was the answer.

"Why?"

"Because it was he who kept us alive during the blizzard; so we wanted to return the favor. That is why we gave him these things."

Then the king asked, "We know that vultures, even being a hundred leagues away from their prey, will perceive a dead body; then why didn't you see the trap set for yourself?"

And the vulture answered with these lines:

When at the end of life
The other-becoming is at hand,
Even a man does not heed this inevitable trap,
Though he eventually will alight there.

When the king had heard this, he asked the merchant, "Is it true, sir merchant, that all these things have been dropped in your courtyard by the vultures?"

"It is true, Sire," said the merchant.

"Where are those things now?"

"Sire, everything has been neatly put aside by me. I shall return to everyone his or her belongings. Please set the vulture free."

So the vulture was given his freedom and the merchant everyone's property.

The Teacher ended this jataka with these words: "The king of the past is Ananda, the merchant from Benares is Sariputta, and the vulture supporting his parents is just I."

– 19 –
The Quail and the Falcon
«Sakunagghi-jataka»

This way I truly learned to love
The boundaries of my natural range.

This tale was told by the Master in the Jetavana monastery. It is about why people often made a connection between himself and the birds.

This was related to the exhortation by the Master: "Monks, do explore your boundaries, but not beyond; stay within the bounds of your own range!"

He made this speech, collected in the Great Section,[22] saying: "So do not go too far. In the days of old, men, still like animals, ventured beyond their own hunting ground, and found themselves in the claws of the enemy. Yet they were able, by efficient use of their wisdom and resourcefulness, to free themselves again."

And he recalled the past.

૭૦

In the past, when Brahmadatta was reigning at Benares, the Bodhisattva, having been born in the kingdom of birds as a quail, maintained himself by pecking between the clods turned over by the plow.

One day he felt the need to roost elsewhere, so he flew to the edge of the jungle, a place where he had never been before. Then a falcon, seeing him seeking food there, whisked down and grabbed him. Clutched tight, hanging beneath the falcon's breast, the quail lamented: "O what a shame! What bad luck is ours! Once we have wandered outside our boundaries into another's range, we are doomed! If we had remained within our boundaries, in our own nativer range, it would not have availed this falcon to attack!"

"What, then, are your bounds, your own paternal range, my little quailie?" asked the falcon, amused.

"The place where the trenches are, made by the plow," said the quail.

Then the falcon released his mighty claws and set him free with the words, "Then go there, you quailie! And you will see that even there you cannot escape me!"

Quickly the quail flew back to his own field, and sat down on a big clod. And he challenged the bird, "Come along now, falcon!"

The falcon braced himself, spread his mighty wings, and at breakneck speed plunged toward the little quail. But when the quail saw him coming—"Good heavens! The falcon is upon me!"—he quickly turned around and hid in a hole behind the clod. The falcon, unable to contain his speed, hurled his breast against it, and so, his heart broken, his eyes protruding, met with his life's end.

And so the quail narrowly escaped death. He came out of his hiding place, stood on top of his pursuer, singing out his emotion: "Aha! The enemy has been beaten!"

And he had learned his lesson:

This way I truly learned to love
The boundaries of my natural range.
Gone is now the enemy, and I am pleased,
Since I am able to see my own luck.

The Master clarified to the monks that, if you fare beyond your boundaries, that is, indulging the desires of the senses, it means giving in to Mara.[24] And in his enlightened state he spoke these lines:

> *The falcon, mightily dropping down—*
> *The quail not even within his own bounds—*
> *Swiftly came upon his victim;*
> *Thereby the falcon met his death.*

The Master then assigned the jataka: "The falcon of then is Deva-datta, but the quail is just I."

– 20 –
The Blessing of Virtuousness
«Silânisamsa-jataka»

Behold the fruits of faith, morality, and generosity. . .

At the Jetavana monastery, the Teacher told this jataka about a faithful layman brother.

One day, this elect disciple who was a convinced believer was on his way to the monastery and by eventide he arrived at the banks of the Achiravati river. The ferrymen had already taken their boats from the water so they could attend the evening service. Because he did not see a ferryboat at the landing to take him across, he took hold of the thought of Buddha as the ecstatic, and in this state he was able to walk over the water. His feet did not sink under water. He just walked there like walking on land, but for one moment, when he saw waves coming in the middle of the stream, his ecstatic Buddha-consciousness weakened, and made his feet sink. Still, he managed regain the ecstasy state, and going along on the water's surface, he reached the other side safe and sound.

Upon entering Jetavana, he respectfully saluted the Teacher and sat down at His feet.

The Teacher welcomed him, looking at his wet feet and asked, "Well, layman brother, did you come here without much trouble?"

"Reverend Sir," he said, "by bringing myself into Buddha ecstasy I could obtain a firm footing on the water's surface, like walking on land, and so I came."

The Teacher said, "Layman, it was not only your remembrance of the Buddha virtues that gave you your footing; in bygone days there were also laymen who, after being shipwrecked on the open sea, were able to walk on water by remembering the Buddha state."

And his listeners insisted he reveal the past.

༄

In days past, during the life of the Very Buddha Kassapa,[25] a converted disciple embarked on a ship, along with a barber who owned some land elsewhere. The barber's wife had recommended this disciple as a traveling companion and committed him to the layman, hoping her husband would have a safe trip.

Unfortunately it was not to be that way. After one week at sea they were shipwrecked, in mid-ocean. The two could save themselves by holding onto a piece of wreckage and eventually they washed ashore on a small island.

Once there, the barber caught a few birds, which he prepared to eat and offered to the layman. But the brother said, "No, not for me!" and did not eat. But then he thought: "In this place I am entirely dependent upon the three refuges,"[26] and he fully concentrated on the benevolent properties. And while he turned inwardly and concentrated, on this islet a *naga*[27], a king cobra, transformed his body into a big ship. A sea deva became the pilot, and the ship was filled with divine energy. The three masts were made of sapphire, the sail made of pure gold, the ropes of silver, and the boarding was golden.

The sea deva, standing aboard the ship, called out: "Anyone for Jambudipa?"

The layman brother said, "Yes, we are!"

"Then come aboard!" said the deva.

He came aboard and gestured to the barber to come, too. But the sea deva said, "You are allowed to come, but he is not."

"Why?" asked the disciple.

"Because he has no moral qualities or conduct, that is why. I brought the ship as an answer to your prayers, not for him."

Then the laymen brother said, "Let him come along; in my own gifts given—my moral code upheld, practice being practiced—I shall give accomplishment to him."[28]

The barber was moved: "Master, thank you!"

The deva said, "Now I shall leave," he made him come aboard, and sailed the ship from the sea up the Ganges, all the way up to Benares. And with his magical powers he deposited money in the houses of both men. As a way of saying goodbye he said, "It is always good to seek the company of the wise. If this barber had not been in the company of this devoted disciple he would have been drowned there, in mid-ocean."

And he spoke these lines:

Behold the fruits of faith, morality, and generosity:
A king serpent in ship's shape brings home the pious layman.
Always choose the right company, make yourselves intimate with
*   the good-hearted.*
By the company of the good this barber owes his salvation.

Thus the sea deva, floating in mid-air above the water, admonished the people who had gathered at the waterside. Then he took the serpent and both of them flew back to their own mansion in the ocean.

The Teacher concluded this jataka with the words: "The devoted layman brother is one who now has passed beyond the wheel of rebirth; the naga king cobra is Sariputta, and the sea deva is just I."

– 21 –
The Jewel Thief
«Manichora-jataka»

There are no gods here! Surely they dwell afar!

This the Teacher taught when living in the Bamboo Wood, about Devadatta's futile efforts to kill him.

When he heard the monks talking about this subject, he said, "Not only today, brothers, but also in the past, Devadatta sought to kill me, but though he strove, he could not."
And he began his tale.

The Bodhisattva once was born in an ordinary householder's family in a village not far from Benares, where Brahmadatta was still reigning.

When he was of age, a daughter from a Benares family was brought to him as a wife. She was lovely, fair, and charming like a divine nymph, graceful as flowering ivy, delicate like a winsome fairy. Her name was Sujata.

She was a devoted wife, sincere and dutiful, performing her duties to her husband, mother-in-law, and father-in-law, and she was dear and charming to the Bodhisattva. And so they lived together in joy and peace; joined in spirit and body.

One day Sujata announced she would very much like to pay a visit to her parents. The Bodhisattva willingly agreed and said, "It is well, my dear, but prepare sufficient food for the journey." And they cooked various foods and placed them in a wagon, preparing for a long and tiring journey. He, driving the wagon, sat in front, and she sat in the back.

Just before they entered the city, they unharnessed the horses and took a bath in the river. Then they continued, again with the Bodhisattva in front and Sujata, who had changed her garment and adorned herself, in the back.

Just when the wagon was entering the city, the king of Benares, sitting on top of his best elephant, was making a tour of the city. And so it happened that the two parties met in that part of the city. Sujata had stepped out to look at the procession, and was walking behind the wagon.

When the king saw her, he could not take his eyes from her. So blinded by her beauty was he that he fell head over heels in love with her. He sent a footman to find out if she was already married. The footman came back with the message: "Sire, they say she is already married. The man in the wagon is her husband."

The king was not able to control his passion for this young woman, and in a matter of minutes he was sick with desire for her. Vicious thoughts played through his mind: "I shall have this man killed by some device, so I can have her. . ." And he ordered his officer, while casually passing the wagon, to drop a jeweled crest into the wagon. According to the king's wish he did this, and when they returned to the palace, he said to the king, "I have done what you asked me to do, Sire."

Afterwards, the king announced, in the presence of everyone: "I just lost my precious jeweled crest!"

And suddenly the whole city was in a commotion. The evil king ordered all gates and passages closed and organized a search party for the jewel thief. Soon, one could see his soldiers searching everywhere in town.

The Bodhisattva's wagon, too, was stopped and the officer ordered, "Sir, stop the wagon; the king's jeweled crest has been stolen and we search search the wagon." And of course the jewel that the officer himself had put there was found. The Bodhisattva was arrested, bound with his arms behind his back, and led before the king: "This is the thief!"

And the king ordered: "Cut off his head!"

The soldiers dragged him through the city to the southern gate, beating him with whips at every crossway.

And Sujata, understanding what had happened, followed him, arms stretched out, and wailing: "My dear husband, because of me this is happening to you!"

The king's men said, "Now we are going to decapitate him." They had the Bodhisattva lie down with his head on the block. When she saw this, Sujata cried desperately: "Alas! It seems to me that in this world there is no god or deity capable of restraining these violent men from harming the virtuous one!"

And in her despair she prayed to the gods:

There are no gods here! Surely they dwell afar!
World peacekeepers are not to be found here anymore!
Those men who precipitately work their lawless deeds—
Is there indeed no one here to bid them to stop?

This righteous woman's lament rose up and radiated around the seat where Sakka,[29] ruler of devas, resides.

Sakka wondered, "Who is this who wants me to leave my domain?" And when he saw what was going on he thought, "This Benares king is being utterly cruel; I should go there and intervene. For his own pleasure he is making this innocent woman an unhappy widow."

And he descended from the deva world, and came down on the back of the royal elephant. He dismounted the wicked king and laid him on his back on the execution block. But he lovingly lifted the Bodhisattva, adorned him with every ornament, and let him take the king's garb. Then he caused him to be seated on the elephant.

When the axe was lifted and a head had been cut off, it was their own king they had decapitated. Only when it was over did they discover what they had done.

Sakka, ruler of devas, took a visible body and went with the Bod-hisattva to the palace, where he was crowned to be king, with Sujata at his side as his queen. When the courtiers and Brahmans saw Sakka they rejoiced and said, "The unrighteous king is dead! Now at last we have a righteous king, named by Sakka!"

And Sakka, floating in the air, warned them: "This is your king now, a gift from Sakka. From now on he will rule righteously. Truly, if there should be any other unrighteous king, the deva will bring rain out of season and drought in season; fear of famine, fear of diseases, fear of the sword of war: these three fears will come upon the earth!"

Thus Sakka gave his warning to the crowd, and went straight back to the deva realms.

And the Bodhisattva ruled righteously and wisely until the end of his days, with his lovely Sujata at his side.

And the Teacher ended this jataka with the words: "The evil king of those days is now Devadatta, Sakka is Anuruddha, Sujata is Rahula's mother, and the Sakka-given king, that was I."

– 22 –
The Arrogant Disciple
«Upahana-jataka»

. . . The ill-bred, shameful man who imitates your teaching
Without his own insight will destroy himself by his arrogance.

This is the Master's story about Devadatta, which he told while staying in the Bamboo Wood.

In the temple, the monks were once more debating about Devadatta's repudiation and openly opposing the Master, bringing himself into big trouble.

To which the Master said that he had done so many times in the past, and he told about such an event.

In the past, when Brahmadatta was king of Benares, the Bodhisattva was born in a family of elephant trainers. He grew up and reached perfection in this art.

Then a young man from a farmers' hamlet came and learned the art from him.

Now elephant trainers have their own, very direct way of teaching, and they do not take no for an answer. So, after the young man had learned the art of training elephants, he said to the Bodhisattva: "Master, I shall now wait upon the king myself."

The king initially offered the lad a half salary (as in the case of Guttila and Musila)[30] and required a test first, in public, before permitting full pay. And so it was arranged.

The Master knew that this pupil was Devadatta reborn, and that he had planned to kill the Master. That is why he decided to teach him a lesson. He thought: "This pupil thinks he has succeeded, but he does not know my skill in strategy yet!"

In one night he trained an elephant to perform the opposite action of every command. In other words, he taught the elephant to stop when he said "Go," to continue when he said "Come back," to lie down when "halt" was said, to pick up when "lay down" was said, and so on.

The next day he mounted this elephant and went to the king's courtyard. The pupil also mounted a docile elephant, and a huge crowd assembled to watch the test ride.

At first, both men showed an equal control in their art. But then the Bodhisattva had them change elephants. And obviously, now the pupil did everything the wrong way, so he blew it completely!

The crowd yelled: "Hey you duffer of a pupil, you dared to compete with your superior! You do not know your place. You are the only one who thinks you are his equal." And they attacked and slew him.

The Bodhisattva dismounted and went to the king. He said, "Majesty, a man learns a trade in order to become happy; but for some the learning of an art leads only to disaster, like a pair of ill-fitting shoes."

And he spoke these lines:

Just like the shoes a man buys
For the sake of pleasure bring but ill;
His soles, oppressed with heat, are chafed,
The feet of such a man are worn;

Even so, the ill-bred, shameful man
Who imitates your teaching without his own insight
Will destroy himself by his arrogance;
Worthless he is called, just like the ill-made shoes.

The king showed much gratitude for the Bodhisattva's teaching and paid him much homage.[31]

The Master ended his anecdote with the words: "Then Devadatta was the pupil, and the trainer was just I."

– 23 –
The One Course
«Ekapada-jataka»

Come! Reveal to me the one course path, my friend...

This parable about a landowner was related by the Teacher during his days at the Jetavana monastery.

This man was living in Savatthi, and he had a son who, while sitting on his father's lap, asked him if he knew what the "gate to happiness"[31] was. Because the father did not know the answer, he went to the Teacher to request an explanation.

The Teacher said, "Not only now, dear layman brother, is this boy an early seeker after weal; in days past he has been, too. He asked wise men and they told him, but because of the confusion incurred by rebirth he does not know now."

And the Teacher recalled the past.

The little boy, seated on his father's lap, asked the wise man: "*Tata*, tell me about the 'one-course path,' which I must go to experience real happiness." He said:

Come! Reveal to me the one-course path, my friend,
*   which I must go,*
That leads to the many ways there are to prosperity
*   and happiness;*
One single way, which encompasses them all, through

which we may
Grow in awareness of what we are all looking for.

The wise father answered him with this verse:

Surrender, in complete knowledge that you are worthy,
That is the single way through which the gates to happiness are
opened;
And this, combined with a sound morality, by patience brought
about,
Will be enough to make friends happy, and sadden foes.

And thus spoke the Bodhisattva with the father about the question of his son. And the son gladly adopted the Teacher's wisdom, lived in prosperity and happiness, and went according to his deeds.

And the Teacher concluded this jataka saying, "The son then is this son now, and the wise father, he was just I."

– 24 –
The Evil King
«Mahapingala-jataka»

Do not fear, he will not return

This is a tale about Devadatta that the Teacher taught at the Jeta-vana monastery.

When Devadatta once had tried for nine months to murder the Teacher and then had sunk into the earth at the portals of Jeta-vana, the inmates and population were very pleased and said: "Devadatta, that thorn in the Buddha's heel, has been swallowed by the earth; finally the enemy of the Enlightened One has been destroyed!" Also the whole population of Jambudipa and the companies of *yakkhas*, elves and devas were very pleased when they heard.

One day the monks were talking about this historical event when the Teacher came into the room. When he heard what they were talking about he said: "Not only now, brothers, but also in bygone times were people happy that Devadatta had died."

And he told about those days.

❧

In Benares reigned, a time long ago, a king named Great Tawny. He reigned without justice or righteousness. He worked evil according to his desires, imposed high penalties and taxes, suppressed the population like sugarcane in a sugar-mill, was hard, rough, violent, and showed no affection or kindness to anyone at all. Even toward the women in his own house he acted unpleasantly and harshly; to his sons and daughters, to ministers, Brahmans and citizens, he was like dust thrown into one's eyes, like stones in alms food, or like a thorn piercing the hand.

In those days the Bodhisattva was born as his son.

After a long reign, the Great Tawny finally died. On the occasion of his death, the entire population of Benares was extremely happy; they cremated him on an enormous mound of logs and they extinguished the pyre with a hundred jars of water.

After that, the Bodhisattva was crowned as the new king. The people jubilated: "Finally, we have a righteous king!" They organized a great festival; the whole town was adorned with brightly colored flags and banners, at each gate a pavilion was erected, with dried and fresh flowers scattered on the floors, and they celebrated with dance, food, and drink.

The Bodhisattva was there, too, seated on a decorated divan in the center of a fine white-canopied dais. Everyone was there: his courtiers and servants, the Brahmans, citizens, officers and gate-keepers, and welcomed the new era with their new king.

But there was one gatekeeper who was standing apart, crying his heart out. The Bodhisattva, who noticed this, summoned him to come near and asked, "Good gate-warden, now since my father has died everyone is having a great time celebrating, and you are just standing there crying; what is the matter? Has my father mistreated you?" And he spoke these lines:

> *All folk were hurt by the Tawny King;*
> *His death creates joy and happiness far and near.*
> *Was the one with white eyes approving your works?*
> *Why is it, gate-warden, that you shed tears?*

Then the gatekeeper said: "I am not crying because of grief that the Great Tawny is dead. Maybe my head is even happy, because the king used to hit my head with blows hard as a smith's hammer whenever he came in and out of the palace. And now that he has gone to the other world, he might be giving these blows to Yama's[33] head and to the hell-wardens. And they will then say 'This is not what we want!' and they will send him back here again. Then he will be giving me more blows on the head; it is from fear that I am shedding tears."

> *Not dear to me was he with the white eyes,*
> *But I fear he might come back again.*
> *In the Beyond, he might even hurt the king of death.*
> *Who, being hurt, may bring him here once more."*

But the Bodhisattva comforted him: "The king has been thoroughly burned to ashes on an enormous pile of wood; the pyre has been drenched with a hundred jars of water and completely covered with earth. Moreover, those who have gone beyond are under the influence of other forces; they will not come back in the same body:"

> *Carbonized with a thousand logs*
> *Is he, then drenched with a hundred jars,*
> *That site is wholly dug over:*
> *Do not fear, he will not return.*

After hearing these encouraging words from the Bodhisattva, the soldier was comforted.

And this king reigned righteously, worked many good deeds for people and country, and was well-liked by everybody.

The Teacher concluded this lesson with the words: "The evil Tawny king then is now Devadatta, and his son is just I."

– 25 –
Guttila
«Guttila-jataka»

I am your refuge, my friend,
I bring honor to the teacher. . . .

While living in the Bamboo Wood, the Master told this story about Devadatta.

On this occasion, the monks were telling Devadatta: "Your reverence, the Very Enlightened One is your teacher. Through Him you have learned the three *pitakas*,[33] and made the fourfold musing arise. It is not fit to become the opponent of your own teacher."

Devadatta repudiated the Master, saying, "What are you saying? The recluse Gautama, my teacher? Didn't I learn and elaborate these things by my own strength?"

The monks were discussing this in the temple and said: "By his repudiation he is calling great disaster upon himself."

The Master came in and heard them talking about this. He said, "Not only now he has repudiated me and become my destructive opponent; also in earlier days he has done so."

And he told about those days.

૭૦

In the past, when Brahmadatta was reigning at Benares, the Bodhisattva was born in a family of musicians, and they named him Guttila.

When he was of age and he had attained mastery in all kinds of musical arts, he became senior musician of all instrumentalists in the whole of Jambudipa. He did not marry, but he did take care of his parents.

In those days, a festival was usually organized for merchants from Benares who were going to Ujjeni to trade, and they, pooling what they wished to contribute, decorated the village with garlands and perfumes, and all kinds of delicacies. They assembled at the sports ground and invited musicians as well.

At that time, Musila was the most famous musician in Ujjeni. They sent for him and made him play. Musila was a lute-player, and he tuned his instrument to the highest possible pitch.

For those who were accustomed to Guttila's artistry , this lute sounded rather like rubbing a rush mat, and none of them applauded. Then Musila thought, "Perhaps I played too high," and tuned the instrument a bit lower. But again, no hands were clapping.

Musila asked, "Good sirs, why do I not please you with my lute playing?"

The answer was rather disconcerting: "Why, were you playing the lute? We were thinking you were still tuning it..."

"What then? Do you know a better expert, or are you not satisfied because of your own ignorance?" asked Musila.

That was an offence to the merchants. They said: "To those who have heard the tones of master lute player Guttila, your tones sound like shrieking women."

Then Musila said, "Well then, take back my fee, I do not want it. But when you go back to Benares, let me go with you!"

They allowed it, and after the festival, when they arrived in Benares they showed him Guttila's place.

When Musila entered the Bodhisattva's house, the first thing he saw was this big, high-class lute hanging there. He took the instrument and played on it. Then the Bodhisattva's parents, who were both blind, said, "Methinks the mice are eating the lute! Shoo! Shoo! Rats are eating the lute!" When Musila put away the lute to greet the parents, they asked, "Where do you come from?"

"I came from Ujjeni to learn the art from the master player," said Musila.

They nodded approvingly. When he asked where the master was they said: "He has gone out somewhere, *tata*; but he certainly is coming back today, to take care of us."

So Musila waited quietly, and in the evening the Bodhisattva came home. After paying this courtesies, Musila told him the reason of his visit. The Bodhisattva had a sixth sense for faces, and he sensed this was not a good man.

He refused: "Go home, dear fellow, there is nothing for you to learn here."

Then Musila grabbed the parents' feet and asked for their intercession. He begged: "Please, make him give me the course!"

The Bodhisattva could not refuse what his parents wished, so he was unable to wriggle out of it, and he taught Musila.

One day, Musila went with the Bodhisattva to the king's palace. The king asked, "Who is he, Master?"

"He is my pupil, your majesty," said the Bodhisattva. And it did not take long before Musila became the king's confidant, and visited him more often.

Meanwhile the Bodhisattva trained him in his own informal, natural way, and when he had taught him all he needed to know about the art, his teacher said, "Well now, *tata*, your course is really finished."

Musila thought, "I now have had an excellent education and this city of Benares is the most important city in the whole of Jambudipa; the Master here is already old, so I ought to stay and live here." And he said, "Master, I would love to play for the king."

The Master said, "Very well, *tata*, I shall tell the king." And he went to the king and said, "My pupil would like to play for your majesty; could you please tell me his fee?"

The king answered: "He will get half of what we usually give you."

When Musila heard this, he said, "I shall play for him if I get the same fee you have, otherwise I shall not play."

"Why is that?" asked the Master.

"Do I not know now as much as you about playing the lute?"

"Yes, you know."

"That being so, why will he give me only half?"

The Bodhisattva informed the king about his refusal, and the answer was: "If he is able to show the same skill and virtuosity as you have, master, then he will receive the same as you."

When the Bodhisattva came home with this message, Musila reacted: "Excellent. I shall show him."

Then it was agreed to hold a competition seven days later at the palace, with the king as judge and jury. The king summoned Musila to the court and asked, "Is it true you wish to compete with your own master?"

"It is true, sire," said Musila.

The king tried admonishing him once more: "It is absolutely not fit for a pupil to contest his master; it just is not done. So give it up."

But Musila insisted, "Enough, majesty, let the competition take place; we shall then find out what we wish to know."

Then the king consented and passed the message around by tom-tom that everyone was invited to hear teacher and pupil compete at the king's gate.

The Bodhisattva thought, "This Musila is still young, almost a child; I am old and wasted. An old man's performance is not very appealing. So if the pupil is defeated, there is not much honor for me to win; if the pupil wins ... well, it would be better for me to go into the woods and die, than to be dishonored."

So he entered the forest, distracted with fear and grief. He kept going back and forth. Back in fear of shame, and forth in fear of dying alone, six long days went by. The grass died where he made his footway.

His despair rose up to the seat of Sakka, who looked down upon what was going on. He thought: "Guttila the master musician is suffering because of his pupil's unseemly behavior; now it behooves me to help him." Swiftly as the wind he descended, stood before the Bodhisattva, and told him who he was.

At first the Bodhisattva hardly could believe what he saw and thought he was hallucinating, after all those days of despair. But then he said, "Deva king, I have gone into the woods out of fear of being defeated by a pupil:"

The seven-stringed lute, the passing sweet,
Lovely tones—everything I taught him.
Now he challenges me to the arena—
Please be thou my refuge, Kosiya!

Sakka heard him out, and then acknowledging his cry of agony, said, "Do not fear; I shall be your shelter and hiding place:"

I am your refuge, my friend,
I bring honor to the teacher;
Your tenderfoot will not conquer you;
It is you, teacher, who will conquer him.

And Sakka continued: "When playing your lute, a string will break; just continue to play on six; on your lute you will not hear the difference. Musila might also break a string, but that tone will fail on his lute; at that moment he will have to admit his defeat.

When you see his defeat, then break all your strings, one by one, and just play on the bare body itself; even with all the strings broken, the sound of your lute will be heard in every corner of Benares city."

Then Sakka handed the Bodhisattva three dice and said, "When the sound of your lute is covering the whole city, throw one die up into the air. Three hundred nymphs will then descend before you and dance. Then throw the second die, and another three hundred will come down and dance; if you then throw the third one, once more three hundred will dance in the arena. I shall be present. Now go, and do not fear."

Very early next morning the Bodhisattva returned home.

At the king's gate they erected a pavilion where they placed the king's seat. Then the king came down from his terrace and sat down on his divan in the midst of the decorated pavilion. Many adorned women, courtiers, Brahmans and countrymen, ten thousand in number,[35] assembled to watch the show. Tier above tier they sat.

And the Bodhisattva had taken a bath and anointed himself with perfumes, and finally ate something. Then he took his lute and went to the palace. He took his place at the king's right-hand side, while Musila sat on the left. Sakka was present in an invisible body; only the Bodhisattva was able to see him.

First both musicians played the same composition, and the crowd responded with loud applause. Then Sakka whispered in the Bodhisattva's ear: "Now break one string." And he broke his B-string; but although the string was broken, it kept on playing the same angelic tone.

Musila also broke a string, but no sound was heard there.

The Master then broke, one by one, the second to the seventh string, and kept on playing on the bare lute neck, while it still brought forth the most wonderful angelic music. The sounds magically spread like incense perfume all over the city; the multitude waved a thousand handkerchiefs; thousands of hands were clapping...

Thereupon the Bodhisattva threw his die into the air, and just like Sakka had predicted, the nine hundred dancing nymphs appeared before him.

Just at that moment the king made a sign to the crowd, and they rose, crying: "You had been warned not to strive against your own teacher, thinking you were his equal. You did not know your measure!"

And the people caught him, stoned him to death, and dragged his body to a garbage dump...

The king was very pleased with the outcome and showered the Bodhisattva with gifts and wealth, and so did the citizens.

Sakka saluted the Bodhisattva gallantly. He said, "Wise Master, soon I shall send Matali down to you in the chariot of victory with the thousand thoroughbreds, and this will bring you here to the deva world."

When Sakka had returned to his throne, the devas asked about his journey. He told them what had happened, praising the good qualities of the Bodhisattva. The devas said, "Majesty, we desire to meet this Master; bring him here!"

Then Sakka ordered Matali to bring the Bodhisattva with the heavenly chariot. When he arrived in the deva world, Sakka welcomed him saying, "Master, the devas are burning with desire to hear you play."

The Bodhisattva replied, "Majesty, we musicians are living by means of our art; we may play where a fee is given."

"Play; I shall gladly pay your fee," said Sakka.

"I do not need another fee than that the devas will talk with me about their own good deeds; for that I shall play."

Then the devas said, "After you have played for us we would love to talk with you about our virtues. Now play, Master!"

For seven days the Bodhisattva played for the devas, and he even surpassed the deva music with his beautiful art. And afterwards, one by one, they told him about the good deeds they did on earth, in the days of the Kassapa Buddha: about a cloak given to a monk; of flowers another monk received; about all kinds of offerings presented to shrines; about hospitality to traveling monks and nuns; about duties done with good temper to a husband's parents; about the sharing of gifts received; about gentleness and generosity in a life as a slave... Thirty-seven devas told him so about their lives and deeds and their rebirths (karma and reincarnation) in verses like those given in the *Vimanavatthu* collection.[36]

After listening to these for another seven days, the Bodhisattva said, "What a delightful way to win! By coming here I have heard more than I could learn in three earth lives. Now I can return to the world of men, and do my good works."

And he breathed this inspired poetry:

Ah, how welcome it is to me what happened to me these days!
Sweet in setting forth, sweet in what was returned!
That I might behold the devas, those comely nymphs.

Now that among them I have heard the Right,
Much worthy deeds will be mine to do:
In gifts, in righteousness, in self-control, and restraint.
I shall go where one knows no grief or pain.

After these seven days, the deva king ordered Matali to take the
Bodhisattva with his chariot back to Benares.

Once returned there, he told everyone what he had seen in
the deva world. And many people were inspired by his words and
deeds, and, full of energy and dedication, trod on the same path.

The Teacher assigned the jataka: "Musila then is now Devadatta,
Sakka is now Anuruddha, the king is Ananda, but Guttila the
musician is just I."

– 26 –
The Judas Tree
«Kimsuk'ôpama-jataka»

Just like the boys and their doubts about the judas tree
In all attained knowledge are aspects unknown

This is a story told by the Teacher while living at the Jetavana monastery. It is about the Sutta[37] of the Judas Tree. This parable goes as follows:

Four monks came to see the Tathâgata and asked him for an exercise. They learned the exercise and each of them went to his own dwelling.

One of them, who had mastered the six spheres of contact, attained the state of arahat;[38] the others, who independently had studied the five aggregates (body and mind), the four elements and the eighteen conditions, also attained this state, by training in *Dhamma nupassana*.[39] They told the Teacher about their different ways of access to sainthood.

Then, in one monk there arose a pondering, causing him to ask the Teacher, "If all these different disciplines lead to one and the same nirvana, why is it that this state of sainthood cannot be attained by everyone?"

The Teacher replied, "Why, brother, is it not the same situation like that in the story of the little brothers who saw the judas tree?" And when the monks asked him about this, he told them the story from the past.

ॐ

In those days, when Brahmadatta was reigning at Benares, he had four sons. One fine day, the sons sent for a charioteer and said, "Good man, we would like to see a real judas tree; please show us one."

The charioteer said, "OK, I shall show you." But he did not show the tree to all four sons at the same time.

First he took the firstborn son on his chariot, brought him to the forest and pointed: "Look there, that is a judas tree," and he showed it at the time when it was bare, with only twigs and buds.

To the second son he showed the tree in the springtime of young verdure.

The third saw the tree months later at its crimson blossom time.

And the fourth son was there at the time of fruition.

When later the four brothers sat together, they remembered their visits to the tree. And of course they had an inspired discussion about the appearance of this tree.

"It looked like a scorched pillar," said the eldest son.

"No, I think it more looked like a banyan tree," said the second sone.

The third son said, "No, no, it was more like a mass of red flesh.

The fourth said, "To me, it was as lovely as a flowering acacia." Since they were stuck in this disagreement, they went to their father and asked him: "Father, what kind of tree is the judas tree?"

Then he counter-questioned, "What do you yourselves think about it?" And they told him about their different views.

The king said, "Now each of you has seen the judas tree, but not one of you has asked the charioteer how it looks in other seasons. That is why you have doubts now."

And these lines were his answer to them:

Everyone could see the judas tree and wonder;
What is it then that you are confused about?
It is because you never asked the charioteer
How it shows itself in other seasons.

❧

The Teacher clarified this parable: "Monks, just like those four ignorant brothers who did not ask questions with discrimination and fell into doubt about the judas tree, you, too, are in doubt about this Dhamma."

And being fully enlightened, he recited:

Just like the boys and their doubts about the judas tree.
In all attained knowledge are aspects unknown.

After the Teacher had related this teaching about the right way, he closed this jataka with the words: "The king of Benares of those days, that was I."

– 27 –
The Dry Well
«Jar'udapana-jataka»

The wealth he has won by digging will be ruined if he goes to far. . .

This story about traders from Savatthi was told by the Teacher when residing at the Jetavana monastery.

They were collecting merchandise in Savatthi and loading it onto carts, to trade elsewhere. Before they left, they invited the Tathâgatha and donated a great gift. They received the moral code, saluted the Master and said, "Reverend Sir, we are about to make a long trip for our livelihood. When we have sold our wares and done our business, and we have returned safely, we shall pay tribute to you again." And off they went.

When they were again on their way back, they saw somewhere in the middle of the jungle an ancient, long worn-out well. They deliberated: "This well has no water anymore, but we are very thirsty. Let us dig it up." While digging they came upon many dumped things, from scrap iron to precious beryl stones. They were very contented with this treasure; they filled their empty carts with the stones and returned safely to Savatthi.

After they had counted their riches they said, "We were so lucky; we shall give a big party." Again they invited the Tathâgatha, donated their gifts during the salutation, and when they were all seated, they told the Teacher how they found this treasure.

The Teacher said, "You laymen are now contented with this wealth. Because you knew moderation you won both wealth and your lives. But in the past, there were also people who were not satisfied and moderate, and because they chose not to listen to the words of the wise, they met their life's end."

And when the men begged him for a story by the fire, he told about those times.

In those days, when Brahmadatta reigned at Benares, the Bodhisattva was born to a family of traders, and he became the caravan leader. After they had collected their merchandise in Benares and loaded their carts to the top, they went with a caravan of traders.

While they were going through the jungle they came across a worn-out well. The traders said: "We want to drink here," and they dug out the well, and while digging they found a lot of iron and the like. Although they had found these valuable things to trade, they were not satisfied, and kept on digging. "There must be something more valuable than this down there," they said.

Then the Bodhisattva reacted: "My good fellowmen! Greed is the root of ruin. We now have dug up a lot of value already; let us be satisfied with this and not dig deeper."

Although they were halted for a moment, they still went on digging.

They did not know this well was haunted by *nagas* in the shape of cobras. The king of these *nagas* lived beneath the well, and now falling stones and sand were ruining his dwelling. So he was terribly angry, and with the hot breath of his nostrils he struck them all, except the Bodhisattva, to the ground, and slew them.

He left his *naga* realm and ordered his fellow *nagas* to fill up the carts with gems. He had the Bodhisattva sit on the first cart, summoned young *nagas* to propel the other carts, and he brought the whole caravan back to Benares. When he had sold the gems and given the yield to the Bodhisattva, he and his other snakes went back to his *naga* domain.

The Bodhisattva used the wealth for gifts to the poor in the whole of India, and at the end of his life he ascended to the Bright World.

৯৹

After the Teacher had recalled this episode from the past, he entered a state of bliss and summarized the story in these lines:

While the traders were digging up a worn-out well,
*   looking for water,*
The men came upon iron, copper, tin, and lead,
Silver and gold, pearls and cat's eyes—lots of them.
But therewith not contented, they went on digging.

With burning breath the fearsome, fiery naga slew them.
Hence let him who digs, not dig too deep; exaggeration brings misery;
And the wealth he has won by digging will be ruined if he goes
*   too far."*

The Teacher concluded this jataka with the words: "The *naga* king then is now Sariputta, and the chief caravan trader is now just I."

– 28 –
The Crab
«Kakkata-jataka»

My lord, I shall not forsake you. . . .
You have been always so dear to me.

This is a story about a woman, which the Teacher told when he was living at the Jetavana monastery.

A landowner from Savatthi went with his wife into the country to collect outstanding rent. When he was about to return with an amply filled purse, robbers assaulted him.

Now his wife happened to be a gorgeous, attractive woman. The leader of the gang desired her, so he made plans to kill the landowner. But the woman, who was a virtuous and devoted wife, fell at the feet of the chief bandit and begged him, "Mister, if out of lust for me you kill my husband, I shall kill myself; I shall take poison or hang myself, whatever it takes . . . but with you I shall never go. Do not kill my husband just like that!"

So the bandit let them go, and both arrived safe and sound in Savatthi. When they came to the Jetavana monastery, they thought: "First we shall visit the monastery and salute the Teacher." They went directly to the pavilion of the "Scented Wood Room," saluted the Teacher and sat down at his side. He asked, "Where have you been?"

"Collecting rent, Reverend Sir," he replied.

"And did you have a good journey?" the Teacher asked.

The landowner said, "On our way, Reverend, we were captured

by bandits, and the leader was about to kill me, but my wife begged him not to, after which we were released. She saved my life!"

The Teacher said, "Disciple, in this life she gave you your life back; in days of the past she has done so for wise men."

And when they asked for a clarification, he related the story.

ॐ

In the past, when Brahmadatta was reigning at Benares, there was a big, golden crab living in a lake high in the Himalayas; that is why they called it the Crab Lake. The crab was huge, the size of a threshing floor. He could even seize and eat elephants. Out of fear of the crab, the elephants did not dare go to the water to eat or drink.

At that time, the Bodhisattva had been reborn as an elephant; he was born as a son of the herd's leader. He grew up to be a wise and strong elephant and he was also very handsome, so it did not take long before he had his own mate.

One day he thought of catching the crab in the mountain lake. He took wife and mother and told his father, "*Tata*, I am going to the lake to catch the big crab."

His father forbade him and said, "*Tata*, you will not be able to do that!"

But when he asked again and again his father said, "Go, do what you want to do, but you will learn."

The Bodhisattva took all the elephants who were living around the lake with him to the Crab Lake and asked them, "When does this crab strike—when you are approaching the lake, when you are feeding, or when you are about to leave from the lake?"

They replied: "When we are leaving the lake."

"Well then, you go down now and feed and drink as long as you wish; I shall be right behind you." And so they did.

When the Bodhisattva was the last to leave, the crab caught him with his claw like a blacksmith gripping a slab of iron with his pair of tongs. His wife did not leave him but kept close.

The Bodhisattva dragged the crab along for a bit, but was unable to shake him off. The crab was dragging the elephant closer to his deadly jaws. In his agony, he cried the cry of the captive and tried to run, leaving droppings as he went. His mate could not bear seeing this and tried to run as well. To let her know he was still on his legs and to stop her running, he said:

Creature with golden horns and stalking eyes,
With skin of bone, baldly floating on the water;
Conquered by him, I cry out my helpless rage.
Do not leave me whom you love so deeply!

Then the wife turned and comforted him:

My lord, I shall not forsake you.
Bull elephant, worn by the years,
Three times twenty, unfaltering you stood;
You have been always so dear to me.

Then she supported him: "My lord, now I shall try and talk with the crab and make him let you go." And she begged the crab:

How many crabs be in the sea,
In Ganges or in Nammada,
Oh, lord of the waters, you are in charge!
Set my lord free, because of I who weep!

While she was speaking like this, the crab was distracted by her lovely feminine voice, causing him to weaken his grasp on the elephant's legs. He did not know what was in store for him. Once freed from the claws of the crab, the elephant lifted his enormous foot and put it down on the crab's back, so his body was crushed. The elephant trumpeted with joy, and all the other elephants gathered to finish the job. The two claws lay broken beside him.

When the Ganges burst its banks, this Crab Lake was filled with fresh Ganges water; when the water subsided, water from the lake flowed back into the river. So it happened that the two crab claws were carried away with the great river. One of them ended up in the ocean; the ten brothers of the king fished the other one out of the river while they were out sporting. And they made a drum out of it, and named it Anaka. The *asuras* (demons) caught the one at sea, and they made it into a drum with the name Alambara. Years later, when they were defeated by Sakka, they left the drum behind on the battlefield and fled.

But Sakka kept the drum for his own use, and this is the drum of which they say: "Thundering like the Alambara cloud."

The Teacher closed this tale with the words: "Then, this laywoman was the elephantwife, and I was the elephant who conquered the crab."

– 29 –
The One Hundred Feathers
«Satapatta-jataka»

Take good care when you meet such a one
Who does not accept the word.

This story about Panduka and Lohita was told by the Teacher at
the Jetavana monastery.

Among the six intransigent monks[40] there were two, Mettiya and
Bhummajaka, who were living near Rajagaha; two others, Pun-
abbasuka and Assaji, lived near Kita Crag, and the last two, Panduka and Lohita, lived near Savatthi at the Jetavana monastery.

These last two monks had the habit of bringing up all kinds of
religious matters for discussion; and thereby manipulating co-
cenobites by telling them: "You are no worse than such and such
because of your birth, clan, or morals. If you do not stand for
your own opinion, others will think they are better than you."
This way they made certain opinions persist, and the quarrels
and controversies continued.

The monks disclosed this to the Blessed One. Thereupon he
assembled all monastics and had these two monks come forward.
They admitted the things they were accused of, and the Master
said, "If this is so, brothers, what you did has a resemblance to
the tale of the hundred feathers."

And he recalled the past.

ॐ

In the past, when Brahmadatta ruled over Benares, the Bodhisattva took rebirth in a village family.

When he reached adulthood he did not earn his living as a
farmer or trader, but he became leader of a gang of bandits, over
five hundred in numbers, and he made a living of burglary and
highway robbery. (Strange, but true; sometimes Bodhisattvas,
although they are supreme human beings, live lives as burglars
or thieves—as a kind of extremity in their rebirths. Some people
say it is a flaw in their constellation in the stars.[41]

It happened that a landowner in Benares had died before he was
able to reclaim an old debt of one thousand *kahapanas* from a
man from the country. When later his wife also fell ill and lay on
her deathbed, she told her son: "*Tata*, your father died while this
debt had not been settled; when I also die that man will not give
his money to you just like that. So go now while I am still alive,
and claim the money."

The son went immediately and indeed was repaid by this
debtor. Yet, before he returned home, his mother died, but out of
love for her son she immediately was reborn in a grown jackal,
who found herself directly on the road her son was taking home-
ward.

At that same moment, the lead bandit lay in wait with his
gang alongside that same road by the jungle, to ambush wayfarers. When the son entered the jungle the jackal jumped up and
down before him, to warn him about these robbers, calling out:
"*Tata*, do not go into these woods; there are bandits who will rob
and kill you!" But he could not understand her jackal language,
so he thought: "This jackal keeps cutting into my path; this surely means bad luck," and he chased her away with clods of dirt
and sticks.

Then came a "hundred-feather" bird, who flew to the bandits
and cawed: "That man there has a thousand *kahapanas* on him;
kill him and take the money!" The young man did not grasp the
bird's words either, and he thought, "Well, this must be a bird of
good luck; now I shall be home soon, safe and sound." He lifted
his hands as a salute and said, "Just keep cawing, friend!"

The Bodhisattva, who was able to understand the language of

wild animals, saw what those two animals were doing. He understood immediately what they meant and thought, "This youth is chasing his mother who is trying to warn him, while he is saluting the bird who wishes him evil. What a fool!"

But the youth just continued his way through the jungle, directly into the hands of the bandits. The Bodhisattva had him seized and bound, asked where he came from and what brought him there.

"Did you get the money?" asked the lead bandit.

"Yes, I did," groaned the young man.

"Do you know what happened to your mother while you were gone?"

"No, master, I do not."

"After you left, your mother died, and out of love for you she became a jackal who kept trying to warn you the whole time. You drove her away and the bird with the hundred feathers was your enemy, the one who asked us to kill and rob you. So he did not bring you luck, but your mother was very good to you. Now take your money and go." And he set him free.

The jackal again jumped up and down before him, but now out of sheer joy. She remained with him the whole way through the woods. Then she stayed behind; she also set him free then, to meet his own, happy life.

Then the Teacher recited these lines:

> *Just like the lad, on his lonely way,*
> *While the jackal prowling through the woods,*
> *Was trying to protect him—*
> *Although he thought she was willing him wrong,*
> *And the ill-willing bird willed him well—*
>
> *Take good care when you meet such a one*
> *Who does not accept the word.*

That they who wish him well have spoken,
And when others praise him for his views,
He is just inflating his risk;
Those others he'd rather call his friends
Just like the youth did to the bird.

After this elaboration about the morals of this story, the Teacher finished with this: "The mother of the youth then is Vasabha, the noble woman; the evil bird is Devadatta, and the leader of the gang was I."

– 30 –
The Beautiful Sujata
«Sujata-jataka»

Sire, these were only teasing digs of a woman suddenly
empowered. . .

This the Teacher told during his stay at the Jetavana, about the lady Mallika of Kosala, king Mallika's spouse.

One day she and the king had an argument. The king was angry with her, because he did not want to recognize her as his first queen.

Lady Mallika thought: "I don't think the Master knows yet about the king being angry with me."

But the Master did know, and he thought, "I shall try tod reunite these two." And early in the morning, he went with bowl and robe, and some attending monks, to Savatthi and had himself introduced to the king. The king took his bowl, let him in and offered him a seat; he gave him and his men water of oblation, and ordered soup and *chapattis*.

The Master held his hand over his bowl and asked, "Majesty, where is the lady queen?"

"Ah, Reverend Sir, what is she to you? Her high position has gone to her head," said the king.

The Master reacted: "Your Majesty, you yourself gave her this high position, didn't you? It is just not correct for you to now suddenly treat her like dirt because she has done something wrong."

Reluctantly the king sent for lady Mallika. When she came in, she greeted the Master respectfully.

He told them both, "It behooves you to become at one with each other." And he emphasized again the essence of concord, and then departed.

Back in the chapel, the monks sat and talked about what he had done in the palace. The Master heard them debate and said, "Not only now, but also in times past I brought them together with one talk." And he told about this event.

In the past, when Brahmadatta was reigning at Benares, the Bodhisattva became his adviser of good and righteousness.

Once, the king stood at the open window and was looking down at the courtyard in front of the palace. At that moment the daughter of a fruit salesman, Sujata, a lovely young girl, came by, carrying a basket full of jujube[42] fruit on her head. She called out: "Fresh jujubes! Fresh jujubes for sale!"

When the king heard her voice, he fell in love instantly, and after he was assured she was not married, he summoned her before his throne and gave her the highest position as first queen. And from the very beginning she was the apple of his eye.

One day, the king was eating large jujube berries from a golden platter, when Sujata teasingly asked from her window what he was eating:

What are those egg-like things, Sire,
Lying on your copper-colored dish?
Blood-red tinted and lovely—
I am asking you: tell me now!

But the king grew annoyed and felt offended. "You little jujube peddler, you daughter of a greengrocer, you dare to say that you don't know what jujubes are, the fruit your own family is trading?!"

The things that you, my lady, once in ragged garb and apron,
Were picking for me, this fruit you know all too well.
By this lie your days of joy are over, your riches gone,
Back you will go now to the place where you will pick jujubes again!

When his advisor the Bodhisattva was informed about this quarrel, he thought, "If there is no one else to bring the king to reason, I shall appease him, because she no longer can be dragged through the mud."

He told the king:

Sire, these were only teasing digs
Of a woman suddenly empowered.
Forgive Sujata, majesty!
Let your wrath cease, chariot lord!

After these words, the king condoned the lady's offence and restored her to her place as first queen. From that time on, they both lived together in concord and understanding.

The Master concluded this jataka saying, "The king of Benares then is the king of Kosala now,[43] and his counselor was just I."

– 31 –
The Wise Son
«Sujata-jataka 2»

Look here! A man from whose heart the dart was drawn—
Disappeared is my sorrow, and I am cleansed.

This tale the Teacher taught while living at the Jetavana monastery, about a landowner whose father had died.

This man was mourning because of his loss, and was not able to stop thinking about his father.

The Master saw in him the conditions for the first stage of realizing the eight *Ariya* paths[44] and went, allegedly for alms, together with a monk in attendance, to the mourning man's house, entered, and sat down. He gave him a friendly greeting and said, "Why, brother, are you still in mourning?"

When the man explained the reason of his sorrow, the Teacher said, "Layman brother, in the past there were also wise men who listened to other enlightened men, and hereby they reached enlightenment themselves. As a result, they no longer grieved anymore when their fathers died."

All who were present in that room begged the wise Teacher to recall the past.

༄

Long ago, when Brahmadatta was reigning at Benares, the Bodhisattva was born as a son of a landowner, and his name was Sujata.

When Sujata had come of age, his grandfather died. From that day on his father was steeped in grief; he took his father's bones from the *ghat* (cremation place) and made a clay stupa in his own garden, placed the bones inside, and from time to time honored the stupa with flowers and the like. Then he meditated and lamented. He stopped bathing or anointing himself with perfume; he did not eat anymore and did not mind his business.

When Sujata, his son the Bodhisattva, had seen this for some time, he thought, "From the moment grandfather died, father has only been overwhelmed with grief. No one else but I can help him through this. There is only one way to make him forget his sorrow."

He went out of the city, and saw a dead ox lying there. He fetched some grass and water, which he put before it, saying, "Come on, ox, eat! Drink!"

People passing by shook their heads and said: "My good Sujata, have you gone out of your mind? Are you offering grass and water to a dead ox?" He did not reply.

The people went to inform his father, saying, "Your son has gone crazy; he is trying to feed a dead ox."

When the father heard this, his grieving for his father gave way to concern for his son. He hurried toward him and asked, "My dear Sujata, what are you doing? Why are you offering food and drink to a dead ox?" And he said:

Why pick in a hurry
Green grass and say: "Eat, eat!"
To a creature already passed away;
To an old, worn-out cow?

Truly not by food
Nor drink will you raise an ox
That has no more to life.
In vain you call on him now,
Like you have lost your own mind.

Thereupon the Bodhisattva spoke:

> *The head is still there, the hooves,*
> *Belly, back, and yes, even the tail*
> *Are still the same—I thought*
> *That ox would rise again.*

> *But of grandfather's head,*
> *Hands, feet, everything is gone.*
> *Lamenting beside a tomb of clay—*
> *What you are doing is like you have lost your mind!*

When the Bodhisattva's father heard this, he thought, "I have a wise son. He knows how to harmonize with this world and the next. He did this to give me a hint that it is enough, now."

And he said, "Dear, wise Sujata, I know the saying: 'all things must pass'; that is why I now shall not grieve anymore. You have showed me in a tender way." And he said these verses in praise of his son:

> *Ah verily! Like a strong candlelight*
> *Sprinkled by water,*
> *So was I, burning with sorrow, quenched,*
> *And he pulled out the dart from my heart,*
> *Chased away my deep grief for my dear father.*

> *Look here! A man from whose heart the dart was drawn—*
> *Disappeared is my sorrow, and I am cleansed.*
> *My distress is over; I shall cry no more;*
> *I hold you in great esteem, my son!*
> *Likewise is the way of the truly wise,*
> *With compassion they draw us from the doldrums of sorrow,*
> *Like you have done now, great soul.*

ॐ

The man who the Teacher told this story to had been listening attentively. And with this insight his grief was also quenched. He was initiated in the first path, and his heart became calm and open.

The Teacher ended this jataka saying, "The Sujata of those days was just I."

– 32 –
The Teachings for the One Who Will Listen
«Karandiya-jataka»

Just like the earth cannot be made flat,
I cannot make everyone accept my views.

This reminiscence, about the General of the Law (*Sariputta*), was given by the Teacher to his audience at the Jetavana monastery.

It is said that the elder Sariputta gave the moral code[45] to everyone who came to him, even to men of poor morals like hunters, fishermen, and farmers, bidding them to live by the code.

Reverence for Sariputta prevented them from contradicting him and they just accepted the code, but they did not keep it—they just went about their own lives.

Sariputta discussed this with his fellow disciples. They said, "Reverend sir, you are giving them the moral code without their own consent; it would be better not to give this kind of folk the code."

Sariputta was unhappy about this. When it had become a point of discussion in the temple, everybody knew: "Reverend Sariputta is said to give the moral code to anyone who simply comes to see him."

The Master came in and picked up the conversation and said, "Not only now, brothers, but also in days of yore he did this the same way."

And he brought up this past life.

❧

In those days when Brahmadatta reigned at Benares, the Bodhisattva was reborn in a Brahman family, with the name Karandiya.

After he grew up, he was placed under the guardianship of a world-famous teacher in the temple. This teacher was then giving the moral code to anyone whom he encountered, from fishermen to townsfolk. Actually, he imposed upon them to accept the code. And although everybody politely accepted, they did not live by it.

His pupils said, "Reverend sir, you are giving them the moral code without their own consent; that is why they break it. From now on, it would be better if you give the code only to those who ask for it." He expressed his remorse, but still he continued doing what he used to do.

Now one day, people came to the temple from a certain hamlet, and they invited the teacher for the purpose of giving alms. And he sent for the young monk Karandiya, and deputed him, saying, "Dear brother, I am not able to go; you go to those five hundred youths and collect the alms; then come back with our share."

The young man departed, and on his way back with the whole group of young Brahmans he saw a huge cave alongside the road. He had the group of five hundred seated in this cave and thought, "Our teacher is still giving the moral code to anyone, even when he is not asked to do so. Now I shall make sure that from now on he will serve only those who ask for it."

He stood between the young Brahmans who were seated there at ease, and lifted a big piece of rock, throwing it deeper into the cave. Again he took a piece of rock and threw it. He kept on doing that, until one of the youngsters stood up and asked, "Teacher, what are you doing?"

But he did not say a word.

Then they hurried to the teacher in the temple and told him about what they had seen. The teacher came, and after he had spoken to the young monk, he said:

You now only throw stones into the forest cave
picking them up from the ground, again and again:
Karandiya, what now is the meaning of this?

As an answer the monk gave his explanation:

Sooth, I would like this mountain, girt by seas,
Made as flat as the palm of a hand—
Hills as well as rocky mountains.
That is why I throw rocks into a cave.

When the priest heard this, he said:

No man alone can do this—
Make this world as flat as a palm.
I guess that, in aiming at this cave alone,
Karandiya, you would spend your whole life.

The young Brahman reacted:

If then I cannot fulfill this task alone—
One man not able to level the whole of the earth—
How is it then, Brahman, that you want to make
All these men of such diverse views follow yours?

The teacher, hearing the words behind his words finally repented,
"Karandiya, from now on I shall not behave that way anymore:

With this parable you, Karandiya, made me realize
In a concise and clear manner,
That just like the earth cannot be made flat,
I cannot make everyone accept my views.

In this way the teacher praised his young disciple.
    And after this wise lesson Karandiya accompanied him to his
home.

૭ઌ

The Teacher looked at his elder. And without speaking a single word, they both knew that he also had gotten the message.

Afterwards, the Teacher concluded this jataka saying, "The Brahman teacher is now Sariputta, but the young disciple, Karandiya, was just I."

– 33 –
The Big Ape
«Mahakapi-jataka»

Whether it is about kingdom, foreign countries, army, or city,
All weal is only to be sought by a king who really understands.

It was during his stay at the Jetavana monastery that the Teacher
told this story about one's duty to family.

In the temple they were discussing the way the Very Enlightened
One himself was taking care of his kin (the Sakyas). The Master,
who had just walked in on the conversation, said, "Not only
today, brothers, but even centuries ago the Tathâgatha acted for
the welfare of his kin."
    And he recalled up the past.

In the past, during Brahmadatta's reign at Benares, the Bodhisattva was reborn among the apes. He grew up to be a strong
and vigorous leader of eight thousand monkeys in the *Himavant*
region. There, on the bank of the Ganges, stood a mighty, fully
foliaged mango tree (some say it was a banyan), soaring up like a
mountain peak. Its sweet fruits with a heavenly flavor were as
large as melons, and from some branches the fruit fell on dry
ground; others fell directly into the Ganges. There was also fruit
that fell close to the trunk, between the roots.

The Bodhisattva, who was eating the fruit with his gang, thought, "There will come a day when those fruits hanging over the water will bring us bad luck." So he took care that his herd ate these fruits first, or threw them away if they were not bigger than kalaya peas.

Yet it happened one day that one big fruit that the monkeys had overlooked because it was hidden by an ants' nest fell into the river and was picked up by a net that the king of Benares had set out as a screen when he was out sporting. That particular day he was there as well, and when the fishermen raised the net and saw the fruit, they showed it to the king because they did not know what it was.

The king asked who might know, whereupon the fishermen asked the woodcutters. The woodcutters said it was a mango. Then the king cut the fruit with a knife, made the woodmen try it first, then ate it himself and shared it with his wives and servants. The mango essence permeated his whole body and he liked it so much that he wanted more! When he was sure from which tree it came, he made the woodcutters create a flotilla of boats beneath the trees, and with the royal household he had a big mango party until the next morning. He placed guards with torches in the boats and around campfires on the banks to watch over them.

When finally everybody had fallen asleep in the boats on the river, the Bodhisattva came with his eight thousand apes, leaping from branch to branch, to eat the rest of the ripe mangoes. The king was awakened by their noises, and when he saw what was going on above his head he had his men get up and sent for the archers, telling them, "Make sure those monkeys do not run away, so surround them and shoot them. Tomorrow we shall eat mangoes with monkey meat."

So they encircled the whole group; the archers stood with their bows and arrows fixed. When the monkeys saw this, they went to the Bodhisattva, and asked, trembling with fear, what they should do now.

Their leader said, "Do not be afraid; I shall save your lives."

After these comforting words, he climbed up a trunk to a long, protruding bough of the mango tree. From this branch he leaped with a huge jump to the other side of the Ganges, and hid behind a bush. The archers, who were waiting for their king's signal, did not notice.

There, on the other bank, the Bodhisattva broke a big bamboo shoot at the root, stripped all its leaves off, tied the one end to the bush, and the other end to his waist. Then he leapt with the speed of a gust of wind, back to the mango tree. He just missed, but was able to grab a lower branch with both hands. Quickly he gave a sign to the gang: "On the double: jump over my back and the bamboo shoot to safety!"

The eight thousand apes saluted him and asked forgiveness for jumping over his back, and then they all ran toward safety.

One monkey from his herd was Devadatta. This rival thought, "Now is my chance to settle with him once and for all!" And he climbed up to a higher branch, from where he with his full-grown body dropped down on the leader's back. The Bodhisattva's heart cracked and he felt a terrible pain rising up. And Devadatta made his way out from there, the last one of the gang.

The king had not gone back to sleep, and he had seen all of this happening. He thought, "This is but an animal, yet he knew how to get his herd away safely, disregarding his own safety." The archers returned home without having fired one shot.

At daybreak the king said, "We cannot let this monkey leader languish there just like that. We shall have to find a way to get him out of the tree and give him treatment."

He made the boats turn downstream and had the Bodhisattva carefully taken down from the tree. He then had him bathed, massaged with fine oils, and enveloped in yellow robes, and gave the Bodhisattva an oiled hide on which to rest.

The king sat down next to him and said:

You yourself have made the way free to pass,
So the others could all cross safely.

Now what are you to them, mighty ape,
And what are they to you?

And the Bodhisattva admonished the king like this:

Sire, it was I, lord of all those apes, leader of the pack,
Who—with pain in my heart and terrified by you,
   tamer of foes—
Hurled myself a hundred times the length of a bow,
And bound a strong shaft of bamboo to my waist.
Like a wind-torn cloud I leaped across to reach the tree,
Failing to alight there, I caught a bough and gripped it with
   both hands.
In my precarious position between bamboo and branch
I made the beasts cross over safely from the tree.

No bondage worries me, nor death;
Weal I brought to those I lead.
This lesson is for you, O king, to mend your ways.
Whether it is about kingdom, foreign countries, army,
   or city,
All weal is only to be sought
By a king who really understands.

Thus taught the Great Being, and then he died.

Then the king ordered his courtiers to organize the obsequies for the ape king as if he had been a king of men. He ordered his women to go, with red garments and flower garlands, disheveled hair, and carrying lanterns on staves, to the funeral as the ape king's retinue.

At the cremation place, the king had a shrine erected, where lamps would eternally burn and flowers and incense were offered. And he had the skull inlaid with gold, added the honored symbol of a spearhead, and paid his respects.

Later on, he took the skull back to Benares, honored it for seven days, while the city was decorated; afterwards he had it entombed in a shrine.

And, purified by the Bodhisattva's exhortation, the king reigned righteously, did many good works, and finally was welcomed into the Bright World.

The Master ended this jataka saying, "Then Ananda was the king, and the monkey king was I."

– 34 –
The Fairy Chanda
«Chanda-kinnara-jataka»

Let us now wander among fresher streams from the rock. . .
And sing to each other our love songs.

When he was abiding in the Banyan Park near Kalipura, the Master told this tale about Rahula's mother.

After the Master first had paid his respects to his father, raja Suddhodana, they went together to visit Rahula's mother. There he praised her virtues and said, "Now I shall tell the parable of the fairy *Chanda*."

Suddhodana first began a song of praise about her virtues: "Reverend Sir, when my daughter-in-law heard that you had adopted the yellow robe,[46] she also dressed in yellow. When she heard that garlands and finery were abandoned, she gave up all of that, too, and even sat on the floor instead of chairs. When you left the world, she became a widow and refused gifts from other rajas. Thus in her heart she is still loyal to you."[47]

The Master said, "Actually it is not phenomenal, majesty, that she in this present life cares so much about me and no other. Even when she had a life in the nonhuman sphere of the fairies,[48] she was." And he recalled the past.

❧

In the past, when Brahmadatta was king of Benares, the Bodhisattva was born in the Himavant region, into the world of the fairies. His wife was called Chanda. Both dwelled on the slopes of a silver mountain, also named Chanda, or Moon Mountain.

In those days, the king of Benares had temporarily handed over his duties to his ministers, put on two yellow robes, taken the five weapons[49] and left on his own for the Himavant.

When he ate some venison he became thirsty. He remembered having seen a small river nearby, so he climbed up toward it.

The fairies who live on Moon Mountain usually stay in the very high regions during the rainy season, and they come down when it is dry. Just then, the Bodhisattva and his wife were coming down the mountain. They were eating pollen, donning and decorating themselves with flowery gear, making creeper-swings and singing with their sweet voices. When they came to the little river, they went down to a dock, where they played in the water, scattering flowers, creating a flower-couch in the sand. Then they picked up a bamboo reed and both sat down by the river. They played flute music through the reed and sang again in their sparkling voices. And Chanda, bending her hands in flowing movements, danced and sang for the Bodhisattva.

The king heard these sounds and crept silently near. He hid when he saw the two fairies, and instantly fell in love with Chanda. He shot the Bodhisattva, so he might carry her off. The poor fairy, wailing in pain, groaned:

Life is passing away, methinks, Chanda—
I am drowning in a pool of blood.
It is life itself leaving me, O my Chanda,
My living breath is ceasing.

Now I am sinking, I feel so strange;
My heart is burning, I feel myself slippinginto darkness.
And it is because thou, Chanda, art grieving,
For this, nothing else, I am grieving, too.

Like grass, like the trees, I perish—
Like a stream, not replenished by the source—
And this is because thou, Chanda, art grieving,
For this, nothing else, I am grieving, too.

Like rain on the lake at the foot of the mountain,
My tears are ever flowing,
And this is because thou, Chanda, art grieving,
For this, nothing else, I am grieving, too.

Thus lamenting, he lay on his flowered couch; then he lost consciousness. The king kept still in his hiding place. And Chanda, initially not aware of what had happened, saw the Bodhisattva collapse. Then she discovered the blood flowing from his wound and, unable to bear the mighty grief for her dear spouse, she started wailing loudly.

The king, who guessed the fairy was dead, then showed himself. When Chanda saw him she thought, "This must be the bandit who shot my dear husband." And she fled quickly, trembling with fear and shock, away from the place of terror. Standing on the hillside, she brought a curse upon the king:

A wicked prince is he who shot my chosen mate,
The mate of my wretched self, lying wounded on the ground.
May your mother repay you, prince, for the grief that is in my heart,
The heartache of longing for my fairy man.
Yes, may your mother get it even with you!
You, who have murdered my fairy man
Only out of desire for me!

Attempting to comfort her, the king said:

Please do not weep, Chanda, grieve not,
You with eyes like the forest timira!
Become my wife, the honored lady in the royal house.

Thereupon Chanda cried like a lioness, "You! What are you telling me?"

> *No, never, I would rather die on the spot,*
> *Than become yours, prince;*
> *You who have murdered my fairy man*
> *Only out of desire for me!*

When he heard her reaction, his passion for her trickled away, and he said:

> *O fairy woman, both timid and life-loving,*
> *Go back to the Himavant!*
> *You, who feed on talisa and tagara,*
> *In the forest the deer will give you joy renewed.*

Then he went away.

When she knew she was safe, she came down again, carried the Bodhisattva in her arms up to the hill, and sat with him, his head on her lap. Her lamentation rose up to the heavens:

> *All these mountains, caves, crags, and rocks,*
> *If you cannot see them, O fairy man,*
> *What shall I do?*

> *All these lovely spots, strewn with flowers,*
> *Haunt of so many a wild beast—*
> *If you cannot see them, O fairy man,*
> *What shall I do?*

> *The clear flow of rivers, sparkling around the rocks,*
> *Streams strewn with blossoms—*
> *If you cannot see them, O fairy man,*
> *What shall I do?*

The blue tops of the Himavant,
And clear skies as far as you can see—
If you cannot see them, O fairy man,
What shall I do?

Gandhamadana, where troops of yakkhas
And fairies live peacefully next to one another
And healing plants are growing—
If you cannot see them, O fairy man,
What shall I do?

Hoarse with grief she placed her hand upon his chest and felt that he was still warm. "He is still alive," she thought, "I shall wait here for an answer from heaven."

And she sent her plea up to the devas:[50] "What now? Are there no protectors of the world anymore, or have they gone to a far-away place, or are they dead, unable to protect my dear husband?"

The keenness of her grief reached the throne of Sakka. When Sakka discerned the cause, he came down in the form of a Brahman, and sprinkled water from a can over the Bodhisattva's body.

Thereupon the poison from the wound evaporated, color returned to his face; the wound vanished, and well and alive, he sat up.

When Chanda saw that her dear husband was alive again, she fell at Sakka's feet, singing:

I worship thee, venerable Brahman, who hast sprinkled my
*   chosen mate*
With ambrosial drops from your celestial water store
And reunited me with my dearest one.

Sakka then advised them: "From now on, remain up there at Moon Mountain and do not descend into the way of men." And then he returned to his throne in the deva heaven.

And Chanda said, "What do we want here at this place of peril? Come, dearest one, let us climb uphill!"

Let us now wander among fresher streams from the rock,
The riverheads strewn with blossoms,
The manifold tree haunts and lakes,
And sing to each other our love songs.

The Teacher concluded this beautiful tale saying, "The king who shot the fairy man is Anuruddha, the fairy Chanda is Rahula's mother, and the fairy man was just I."

– 35 –
The Spell of Beauty
«Ummadanti-jataka»

Truly, she had but glanced at me
And Ummadanti turned me into a madman!

At the Jetavana monastery, the Master told this story about a love-sick monk.

One day, when he was going about Savatthi for alms, he saw this exceptionally beautiful woman in attractive garb. He fell in love with her and was unable to think of anything else. He returned to the *vihara*,[52] and from that moment on, he was sick with passion, as if hit by the proverbial love arrow. He resembled a maddened deer, lean, his limbs awkward, as if entangled in a net; his face became ever sallower, and he cared for nothing else. He could find no peace in any kind of meditation, and was absent from studies, prayers, and exercise...

To the other monks who expressed their concern, he invariably said, "I do not care!"

They reacted: "But you should care! It was hard enough to choose this kind of life as it is. That part of the battle you won already; and to end all sorrows you said goodbye to your family and the common world in faith. Why then do you allow yourself to be wrapped up by these passions for a woman?"

And they brought him before the Master in the temple.

"Brothers, why did you bring this monk to me against his own will?" he asked.

"Because we heard he is hankering after a woman," was their answer.

The Master asked, "Is this true?"

"Yes, Reverend Sir, it is so."

"Brother, in early days there were sages who, even while they had a whole kingdom under their command, or even when they came under the spell of someone or something, they were able to contain themselves, doing nothing unseemly."

And he told a parable about this.

৯

Once, in the past, a king was reigning in the city of Aritthapura, in the kingdom of the Sivis, and the Bodhisattva, who was born as a child of this king and his first wife, was also named Sivi.

To the captain of the king's army a son was born as well, with the name Ahiparaka.

Those two boys grew up together as comrades, and when they reached sixteen they went to Takkasila to learn the martial arts; and when they had learned enough, they returned to their hometown.

In due time, the king left his kingdom in the hands of his son, and Sivi appointed Ahiparaka as his commanding officer. And the new king ruled righteously.

Now in this city lived a rich man, Tiritavaccha, who had many millions. His daughter was exceptionally handsome and sweet, bearing auspicious features, and on her naming day they called her Ummadanti. At sixteen she had an angelic appearance, almost like a blonde deva nymph; every man who saw her was spellbound by her breathtaking beauty, as if he were completely drunk, losing his presence of mind.

Then her father appealed to the king, saying, "Sire, under my roof a jewel of a woman has grown, fit to become a queen. Please send feature augurs who can test her, then do with her as you see fit."

The king agreed and sent Brahmans to the millionaire's house. They were all well-entertained with rice milk and sweets.

Then Ummadanti appeared in the doorway, charming in all her features. At once, when they saw her, they almost fainted and completely forgot they were sitting at their host's table. Some of them could not even bring the food to their mouths anymore; it ended up somewhere over their heads or against the wall. They were completely entranced.

When she saw them there, losing their composure, she said,"Well, are those the men who were supposed to examine my features? Grab them by their collars and show them the door!" And so it happened.

Confused and vexed with her, they went to the king's residence and declared: "Sire, that woman is some kind of a witch; she certainly is not fit to be your queen."

When the king heard this, he did not bother to send for her.

When the girl heard what the men had said about her, she commented, "So I have not been chosen by the king because it seems I am a witch? So now I know what witches are like!"

And she brooded on some kind of plan to get even with them. She thought: "All right, so be it! Only when I am standing eye to eye before the king, shall I know for sure."

Her father was of course very disappointed that the king showed now interest in his daughter. So then he gave her away in marriage to Ahiparaka; and she was dear and charming to him.[51]

In Aritthapurat, at the end of the rainy season, a big festival was arranged, with sacrifices to the rain devas, and by the time of the full moon, the whole city was decorated.

Ahiparaka, who was going to his place of work at the office of warding, advised his wife: "Dear one, today is the rains-end festival; the king will make his lucky tour through the whole city and he will pass our house, too. Do not show yourself to him; for if he sees you he will lose his bearings completely!"

When he had left, she thought, "Now will be the moment I shall know for sure!"

She told the female servant,: "When the king is passing this house, let me know."

And at sunset, when the city looked like a deva city, with lanterns burning everywhere, the king, in brave, resplendent attire, in his best chariot with thoroughbreds, surrounded by his officers, made his tour.

Then he passed Ahiparaka's house. A beautifully decorated red brick wall with a huge gate surrounded this house. The servant warned Ummadanti that the king was coming, so she went to the balcony, angel-like and adorable, and threw flowers to the king. When he looked up at her, he was instantly intoxicated with passion for her. Unable to keep his presence of mind, he did not recognize he was at his best friend's house. So he asked his charioteer:

Who would be owner of this house, Sunanda,
Protected by this bright-colored wall?
Who is it I see there like a radiating light,
Aloft in the air like a flame on a hilltop?

Daughter of whom, Sunanda, may she be?
Whose daughter-in-law, or is she married yet?
Quickly, tell me now what I ask you,
Is she still free, or has she bonds in marriage?

The charioteer answered:

Truly, I know her, lord of men,
Both the mother and the father,
And also her husband, O guardian of the land;
Successful is he, prosperous and rich.

By day and night in harness for your merit
He is one of your truest ministers, O lord of men;
Spouse of Ahiparaka is she,
And Ummadanti is her name.

When the king learned this he promptly reacted:

O master charioteer, is this her name?
Very well chosen by mother and father!
Truly, she had but glanced at me
And Ummadanti turned me into a madman!

When she saw how agitated the king had become upon seeing her, Ummadanti closed her window and went to the summer-house in the garden. Because the king, after having seen her, could not possibly finish his tour through town, he told the charioteer to turn the wheels and said, "This festival is not ours; it belongs to captain Ahiparaka." And he turned back to the palace, where he secluded himself in his own quarters. He could not think about anything else but her.

The officers told Ahiparaka how the king had turned around at the gates of his home. Arriving home, he asked Ummadanti: "Dearest, did you allow the king to see you?"

She answered, "Dear husband, someone passed by in a chariot, with a big paunch and big teeth. I do not know if he was the king or someone else from the court—someone in authority they said—and I was just throwing some flowers out of the window when he passed by. He then turned and went away."

When Ahiparaka heard this, he moaned, "Now I am dead! You have destroyed me!"

Early the next morning, he went to the royal dwellings and when he stood at the door of the king's room, Ahiparaka heard him mumbling to himself about Ummadanti and he thought, "Now he is head over heels in love with Ummadanti; if he does not get her, he will die. If I am to save myself and the king from doing insane things, I shall have to save his life."

He went back home again, summoned a strong attendant and told him, "Friend, you will go to that big hollow tree near the temple. Go there secretly, let nobody see you, and hide inside the tree. I shall then go there too, to bring offerings, and when I shall invoke the tree deva I shall pray: 'O deva king, our king does not want to celebrate with us. He is just lying in his bed, talking to himself. We do not know why, because the king was always a benefactor of devas, spending a thousand or more on sacrifice. Could you tell us why he is doing this now, and could you also see to it that he lives?' Then you have to learn the following words by heart and tell them with a deva like voice: 'Commander, your king is not ill, but he has fallen in love with your wife Ummadanti. If he wins he,r he will live; if not, he will die. If you want him to live, you will have to give Ummadanti to your king. . .'"

Like this Ahiparaka instructed his servant and sent him away. He also informed his officers to accompany him to the temple. After invoking the tree deva, Ahiparaka made sure his officers heard the words from the voice in the tree.

The officers then went to the king and told him about this, making the king even more bemused.

Later that day Ahiparaka went to the palace once more, and knocked at the king's door. The king cleared his throat and asked, "Who is it?"

"It is I, sire," answered Ahiparaka. The king let him in, and upon entering, Ahiparaka saluted and said:

From the world of spirits, who worship their lord,
A yakkha came to me, and this is what he said:
The king has set his heart upon Ummadanti;
I shall give her to you; make her your handmaiden.

The king said, "My good Ahiparaka, I just heard. Do even the yakkhas know now of my gibberish, because I lost my heart to her?"

"Yes, sire."

He felt ashamed and said, "Now the whole world knows how shameful my behavior is!"

And at the same time he apologized:

Fallen from merit, immortal I am not!
The people will learn about this evil deed of mine...
Also within yourself, you will be upset
If you would see your dear wife no more.

The two now got entangled in a heated discussion.
Ahiparaka emphasized his self-sacrifice:

You are to me both father and mother,
Partner and master, protector and god.
I am your servant, yours with children and wife,
As it may please you, Sivi, do as you like.

The king protested:

Whoever substitutes his woe for another woe,
Or with his weal takes another's weal,
It will not be I! So by any means.
Everyone now will know that I realized what is right.

Not even if I could win immortality by doing this wrong
Or have the whole world at my feet—
Even then I would know this is the unjust way
For me, strongest among the Sivis.

As a leader, sovereign, kingdom's guard,
Cherishing the standard (dhamma) *of the Sivis,*
Thus I shall do right to my intention
And not fare by passion of my heart.

Finally, Ahiparaka advised his king:

Surely you, my king, in whom there is so much wisdom,
Will enjoy a long, happy, and lasting reign.
We hail you, who chooses the right path,
Leaving behind your negligence.
Now you choose the right path of your forefathers, noble king!
By choosing this way you will enter the Bright World.
Choose right to the Bright World with children and wife!

Thus his friend Ahiparaka taught the king the right way, and the king brought his infatuated heart into subjection.

And the two friends remained soul mates as long as they lived.

After the Master had narrated this story he concluded the jataka: "Sunanda, the charioteer, is now Ananda, Ahiparaka is now Sariputta, Ummadanti is now Uppalavanna, and king Sivi, that was I."

– 36 –
The Six-Rayed Tusker
«Chaddanta-jataka»

Eight thousand elephants guard him,
With plow-pole tusks, ready to strike.

This is a story about a young nun, which the Teacher told while staying at the Jetavana monastery.

This daughter of a Savatthi family saw the dangers of domestic life for spiritual practice, so she chose a life of seclusion in the monastery.

The first time she went with the other nuns to the Righteous One to hear his sermons, and she saw him with the Ten Powers, sitting in his decorated pulpit, in the supreme beauty of his infinite merit, she wondered: "Have I ever been this man's handmaiden, on my way to liberation, and did I ever love him in ages past?"

At the same moment a memory about a previous life arose inside of her: "I was indeed, in the time of the Six-rayed Tusker."

And a euphoric rapture arose in her, breaking through like a sun ray through the clouds.

She thought, "There are but a few handmaidens who were well disposed to their masters; there are many more who are not. How was I toward my master?"

And then she remembered clearly how she, with ill will, made the hunter Sonuttara hunt the Six-rayed Tusker, the great lord of elephants, a huge animal. The hunter wounded him with a poisoned arrow, which killed him.

By this memory the nun was torn with grief. She could not bear the pain, and gasping and panting, she wept loudly.

The Master looked at her, and he broke into a big smile. When the monks asked him about this he said, "Brothers, this young nun is crying, because she remembered a wrongdoing she once did to me, in a past life."

And he told the whole story.

ॐ

In bygone days, near the Himalayan Six Tusker Lake, there dwelled eight thousand magical elephants who could fly through the air.

Then the Bodhisattva was born there as a son of the lord of these elephants. He was entirely white, except for his red feet and mouth.

Once full-grown, he stood eighty-eight hands high, and one hundred and twenty cubits in length; his trunk was like a silver rope fifty-eight hands long; his tusks, fifteen hands round, thirty hands in length, had six colored rays.[52] Then he himself became lord of the eight thousand. He had two chief consorts: Subhadda Minor and Subhadda Major, and they all lived together in the Kancana ("Golden Cave").

The Six Tusker Lake has crystal clear water in the center, surrounded by a ring of lotus flowers, then a ring of various fruit trees, paddy fields and other trees, then a zone of bamboo wood, changing into seven mountain ranges, all of which has been described in the *Samyutta* commentaries.[53] To the northeastern side of the lake stood a huge banyan tree; to the western side was the Kancana.

One day the news came that the great damar wood[54] was blossoming. The great elephant went along with his herd to that forest, and announced that they would play the "damar-game" over there. With his forehead, he hit a damar tree full of blossoms. Subhadda Minor stood against the wind, and onto her body fell a shower of dry twigs, old leaves and red ants. But Subhadda

Major stood leeward, and her body was adorned with blossoms, pollen, stamens, and young leaves.

Subhadda Minor thought, "Look now with what he serves his dearest, and with what he fobs me off. Go on! Rub it in!"

And anger grew in her toward the Great Being.

Another day the elephant king went with his following to bathe in the lake, and two young elephants took bunches of usira root to wash him down. After he got out of the lake, they washed the two queen elephants, who then came out and stood beside him.

Then the rest of the herd went into the water and played splashing games, and adorned their king and queens with petals. One elephant found a bit further down the lake a splendid seven-headed lotus, and he brought it to the Great Being. Taking it with his trunk, he sprinkled pollen on his own forehead, and then gave the lotus to Subhadda Major. The other queen saw this, of course, and her anger grew even more.

Thent, while the Bodhisattva was busy doing other things, she went to a lonesome spot and sent up a prayer: "When I die now, may I then be reborn in the Madda king's family as a handmaiden with my name, Subhadda. When grown, may I become the first queen of the king of Benares! May I be gentle and affectionate to him and allowed to do what I want. May I then send a hunter who will shoot and kill this elephant with a poisoned arrow; and then bring me his twin tusks with the six colors as a trophy."

From that day on she stopped eating, and she died soon after. . .

She was reborn to the life she had prayed for, and she became chief lady of sixteen thousand women. She also remembered her previous life and her wish.

She thought, "My prayer has been heard; now I shall get those twin tusks."

Then she smeared rancid oil on her body, put on some dirty clothes and, lying down in her bed, pretended to be very sick.

The king came to see her and asked, "Where is Subhadda?"

When he was informed of her illness, he went to her bedroom and sat down on the bed. He gently stroked her back, singing:

Why do you grieve, my graceful one?
Pale like a sheet has my dearest lady grown;
My wide-eyed woman is wilting away
Like a garland crumpling in the hand.

She heard him sing and said:

A sick longing, sire, came over me,
Overwhelming me in my dreams.
Because no easy thing it is that I want,
What I wish for with all my heart.

The king again answered in a sweet song:

Whatever someone ever wishes in this world,
In pleasantries big or small,
All these are mine in abundance;
So whatever you wish, I shall give you."

The queen was all ears now and said, "Majesty, the thing I long for is so hard to obtain. I shall not tell you now yet, but do assemble all the hunters from your kingdom, then I shall explain in their presence."

Sire, let trappers come together here,
As many as there are in your kingdom;
To you and those hunters I shall reveal
What it is I so greatly long for.

The king consented and ordered his officers to summon, with the tom-tom drum, all hunters to the palace. And soon the first hunters from the Kasi kingdom arrived at the palace, glad with any assignment they could have, and had their presence announced to the king. In the end, there were sixty thousand of them gathered at the palace gates!

The next day the king stood on the front steps and addressed the hunters. He pointed them out to the queen and said:

> *Here, my lady, are your hunters and trappers, experienced*
> *   and brave,*
> *Wise in woodcraft, wise in the hunt; I command them unto you.*

Then the queen addressed them directly:

> *Men of the hunt, listen to me all, as many as are gathered here!*
> *Great, white, and with six-colored tusks is the elephant in*
> *   my dreams.*
> *His tusks I want; without those my life has no meaning.*

A spokesman of the hunters stepped forward and said:

> *Never did our forefathers see or hear*
> *Of there being an elephant with six-colored tusks.*
> *What was it in your dreams, king's daughter, that you saw;*
> *Explain to us what kind of animal it was.*

Then the hunter inquired in which part of the country she had seen the elephant in her dreams.

Then Subhadda let her gaze move over all those hunters. Among them she saw one, who was noticeable among all others: broad-footed, big-ribbed, thick-bearded, brown-whiskered, scarred, unsightly, repellent—a hunter who was in past times the Great Being's enemy, Sonuttara.

She thought, "This is someone who will be able to carry out my instructions."

She got the king's permission and took him to the top floor of the seven-storied palace. She pointed toward the north, to the Himalayas, and said:

From here, straight to the province in the north;
When you have passed seven ridges vast,
There rises the high ridge of the Golden Brae,
The flowery haunt of rough woodmen.

When you then climb the crest where fairies dwell
And look down to the foot of the mountain,
Then you will see, many-colored like a cloud,
A king banyan tree, with eight thousand branches.

There lives the Six-Rayed Tusker,
All white, and unconquerable.
Eight thousand elephants are guarding him,
With plow-pole tusks, ready to strike.

Trumpeting and snorting they stand,
Their cries sounding like an imminent warning;
But if someone should come near,
They will blast him away, never to be seen again!

Hearing that, Sonuttara lost all courage and he said, mortally dismayed:

Truly, you have everything in this palace,
Ornaments wrought in fine gold, my queen,
Pearls, jewels, and cat's eye gems.
What will you do, then, with ivory ornaments?
Or is it you just aim at sending hunters to their deaths?

And the queen answered:

Look at me, filled with grudge and deeply afflicted;
And sorely I wilt by remembering.
Do this for me, O hunter man,
And I shall endow you with five villages of your choice.

And she assured him: "Good hunter, I once burned an offering to the Buddha and prayed: 'I wish that, after I have had this elephant killed, his twin tusks will be brought to me.' This is not something I just saw in a dream; but the prayer I offered will come true. Go now and fear not."

He then consented and asked, "All right, tell me exactly where he lives."

Where does he stay? Where does e stand?
Along which path does he go to bathe in the lake?
How does the king of elephants bathe?
How shall I find the trumpeter's tracks?

By her clear memory of her past life she recalled the image of what she had seen, and described it like this:

Just where the lotus pond is near,
Lovely and fordable and filled with blossoms,
The haunt of countless bees;
It is there the king elephant takes his bath.

After his bath his head is crowned with lotuses,
And white all over he rises up from the water;
Joyously he returns to his abode,
Followed by his first spouse, "The One Who Gets It All."

Sonuttara said, "Very well, lady, I shall kill the elephant and bring you the tusks."

Overjoyed, she gave him a large advance, and dismissed him: "First go home, and set out on your mission after a week."

And she sent for a smith, and ordered him to quickly prepare an axe, a spade, a chisel, a hammer, a bamboo cutter, a sickle, an iron staff, stanchions, and a three-pronged grappling iron. She also sent for a saddler to make her quickly a leather sack capable of containing a *kumbha* (a kind of bucket), a leather rope, straps, gloves, and shoes, and finally also a leather umbrella.

All of this was soon delivered at her door.

After a week, when the hunter was due to leave, she had provisions prepared, and all the other requisites for his long journey. And when she had stowed everything into the leather bag, the journey could begin.

After Sonuttara had made his own preparations he left on the seventh day. First he waited on the queen. She said: "Everything you need on this journey stands ready. Take this bag."

And he, as strong as five elephants, lifted it up as if it was a bag of sweets, and slung it over his back so his hands could be free.

While he was gone, the queen would take care of his wife and children, and she informed the king that he had left.

The hunter mounted a chariot, and with a great escort, departed from the city.

He passed through towns and villages, and having reached the border, his escort was replaced by some border folk who guided him into the forest. When they had reached the end of man-made pathways, he turned the others back and went on alone.

Over two hundred miles he worked his way through seventeen kinds of jungle, reaping and chopping a passageway, felling trees and digging out roots.

In the bamboo jungle, he made a kind of ladder, climbed high into a tall bamboo cluster and then swung himself and all his gear from stem to stem. In the marshy area, he took two planks and laid them down one after the other as he went; and in order to cross a watery area he made a canoe from a hollow tree. Finally, he reached the foot of a steep mountain precipice.

Here he tied his grappling iron to his leather rope, and threw it aloft over a rock, allowing him to climb up easily. On other occasions, he drove his diamond-tipped brazen staff into the rock, and then hammered a stanchion into the cleft. Stepping onto this, he hauled up his grappling iron and again hooked it aloft. That way, Sonuttara managed to climb all the way up to the top, with all his heavy equipment. And in a likewise manner he manoevered himself down the other side: he hammered a stanchion at the top of the first ridge, wound his rope around it, and fastening his bag onto it and sitting on his bag he went down, like a spider paying out its web. Some say he glided down with his umbrella, descending like a bird.

The same way he crossed another six mountain ranges, the last and the toughest being the glorious peak, Golden Brae. And finally, from the Fairy's Rock he looked down on the foot of the mountains to the valley, and saw afar the great banyan forest, with its thousands of pillared stems and crowning foliage like one big green cloud.

It took him seven years, seven months, and seven days to reach the domicile of the Great Being. When the hunter finally had discovered this domain he decided to dig a deep pit in order to trap the lord of elephants in it.

He went into the forest and cut down trees for girders, and strewed a heap of grass. And when the elephants left to bathe in the lake, he dug a deep, square pit in the ground with his great spade, and he sprinkled the soil he had dug out with water. Having set up props in the pit on mortar stones and given them weights and ropes, he laid planks on top of them. He made a slit the size of an arrow, and after he made a small entrance for himself at one side, he scattered soil and leaves on top of the trap.

When the trap was made, he tied a false topknot on his head, donned yellow robes, took his bow and poisoned arrow, and descended into the pit.

And the Teacher summarized what happened next in these verses:

Making a pit, with planks the hunter covered it;
Then he crept inside with his deadly bow,
Marking the coming elephant, the merciless ill doer
Shot only once
With poisoned arrow.

The wounded elephant trumpeted loudly,
And all the elephants roared like a menacing thunderstorm,

Crushing grass and brushwood to dust,
Then ran away into all directions.

Planning to slay the man who attacked him,
He then saw his yellow robe, the sign of seers!
Smitten with pain the thought arose in him,
The sign of a saint, of the good inviolate...

He who suffers vice, yet dons the saffron robe,
Keeping afar from self-control and truth,
How unworthy he is to wear the saffron hue.

He who rejects vice, steadfast in his virtuous ways,
And yokes himself to self-control and truth,
Worthy is he to wear the saffron hue.[55]

With these words the Great Being banned the thoughts of anger or hatred toward the hunter and he asked him, "Good man, why did you hurt me so badly, for your own reasons, or are you employed by someone else?"

Thereupon the hunter answered honestly:

The queen of Kasi's majesty, my lord,
Subhadda—she summoned me at court.
She had seen you and directed me;
She wants your tusks, so she said.

When he heard her name, the Great Being knew instantly this was the work of Subhadda Minor. He endured his pain and explained to the hunter, "She does not have it in for my husks; she sent you to murder me."

And he spoke these verses:

A wonderful pair of tusks are my boon,
So are those of my sires and grandsires;
Know that the angry king's daughter
Wanted me dead, and caused this entire pointless struggle.

Get up, you hunter, take your hone,
Cut off these tusks, before I die;
Tell this to that angry king's daughter:
"The beast has been slain, look here—his tusks."

Then the hunter immediately got up, honed his saw and approached the elephant. But he was of such a great height that his tusks were out of reach. Then the Great Being stooped and lay down, lowering his head. And the hunter, climbing up on that silver trunk, stood on the forehead as if on Kelasa's peak, and prepared himself to put the saw to one of the tusks. But he only sawed into the mouth of the beast. The Great Being was in pain and his mouth was filled with blood. The hunter shifted his saw up and down but was not able to get the job done.

Then the Great Being emptied his mouth, endured his pain and asked: "What now, good man, are you not able to cut it off?"

"No, master, I cannot," said the hunter.

The Great Being kept his presence of mind and said: "Well then, lift up my trunk, so I can catch the end of the saw; I do not have the strength to lift it up myself."

Then the Great Being took hold of the saw with his trunk, and worked it to and fro and cut off his tusks, as if they were twigs. He presented them to the hunter, saying: "Good trapper-man, I am giving you my tusks, not because I do not care, nor for any sacrifice for higher gain myself, but because the tusks of the knowledge of all-that-is are much dearer to me than these. May this merit be the cause of knowledge of all-that-is!"

And then he asked, "My man, how long did it take you to come here?"

"Almost eight years," said the hunter.

Then the great elephant said, "Go; by the powers of these tusks you will reach Benares within seven days."

As he dismissed the hunter, he gave him a protective amulet to wear around his neck. Then the Great Being died a little later, in the midst of his Subhadda and other loved ones.

After the hunter had left, the elephants all came back. Together with Subhadda they all cried heartrendingly about the loss of their great leader, and their wailing rose up to the lonely Buddhas, neighbors of the Great Being: "Reverend beings, the Great One has died, wounded by a poisoned arrow; please come and attend his funeral."

And the five hundred lonely Buddhas, floating through the air, came down from the heavens and formed a floating circle above the elephants. At that moment, two young elephants lifted the body of the elephant king with their tusks and laid it on the pyre. The lonely Buddhas paid their respects, and then the body was cremated, while the lonely Buddhas recited prayers all night long at the crematory. After the eight thousand elephants put out the fire and bathed in the lake, they returned to their abode, with Subhadda leading.

Sonuttara reached Benares before the seventh day, with the tusks. In the city, he attracted a great deal of attention with the six-colored tusks.

Presenting himself at the court, he stood before the queen and said, "Lady, he, for whom you nursed so much hatred in your heart, has been slain by me. He is dead."

She answered, "That is what you claim, that he is dead."

"Look for yourself, here are his tusks," said the hunter.

With a jeweled fan in her hands she inspected the beautifully colored tusks. When she saw the tusks, with a shock the remembrance came back to her of him, who had been her mate in her previous existence. And she said, "After the hunter with a poisoned arrow ended the life of this beautiful elephant, he came here to offer his tusks as evidence."

Unbearable grief arose in her; then her heart broke. That very day she died.

And the Teacher concluded the story in a song:

The Enlightened One, the Mighty One
Smiled in the midst of their company.

The monks asked him:
So Buddhas do not show themselves without cause?

The young woman you saw crying today
Was the elephant queen, who felt rejected,
And thereafter she was the king's daughter.

I then was the elephant king.
The hunter-man who took the tusks
Of the incomparable trumpeter—
Such magnificent colors, unmatched on earth,
They were—and he brought them to the Kasi city,
Devadatta himself, that was he.

This world-old faring, high and low,
This long procession of the nights
On which the sun yet does not set:
He from whom pain and grief had fled
And hunter's dart, he of the things
Himself knew well, the Buddha told.

In those days I was for you, yeah you, brothers,
Your elephant king, loyal to all;
So now there is something for you to learn here,
The lesson from this story of a former lifetime.

The elders, reciting the Dhamma and praising the virtues of the
Ten-Powered One, recorded these verses.

Notes

1. See jataka 11.
2. *Tathâgatha* – the perfected one, an epithet for the so-called transcendental Buddha, also named Jina (victor) or Dhyani-Buddha (meditation Buddha). The Buddha used this word when referring to Himself. Literally, *tatha* and *gata* mean: "He who went all the way" or "he who attained the truth" or "he who understands things as they are."
3. Savatti – the modern Sahet Mahet, a town with the oldest historical tree, which can still be visited. This is the tree that Anathapindika had planted so people could honor the Buddha when he was not around. Because the organization handling the planting of the tree was owned by Ananda, the tree was named "the Ananda Bodhi tree."
4. *Dhamma* – the right way or straight path; in Buddhism this is equal to "that which ought to be."
5. *Tata* – a pet name, so here it would mean something like "dear boy."
6. The one who has cut the ten ties (binding us to this world, *saññojana*): 1. beliefs of personality; 2. doubts; 3. attachments to rules and rituals; 4. sensual passions; 5. hatred; 6. longing for non-material existence (not being in the body, taking drugs, etc.); 7. longing for (life after) death; 8. arrogance; 9. restlessness; 10. ignorance.
7. The king's first and most important wife; the king used to have several wives.

8. This is an interesting expression here, rarely found in Buddhist scriptures; it is more Brahman than Buddhist.

9. The higher realms, heaven. According to the Buddhist and Hindu religion, *devas* are heavenly beings who are living in blissful worlds or spheres, and who usually are invisible to the human eye.

10. Meaning she has had thirty two lives before.

11. It reflects little credit on the composers of this story to describe Gautama here as someone who was led by things others might say or think of his behavior. The origin of the story may well have been only a few legendary outlines, which through the ages evolved to a complete history.

12. *Sila Sikkha* – the moral directives basically consist of five rules (or intentions): I resolve to train myself not to kill (*panatipata veramani sikkhapadam samadiyama*), I resolve to train myself not to steal (*adinnadana veramani sikkhapadam samadiyama*), I resolve to train myself to refrain from illicit sexual intercourse (*kamesu micchara veramani sikkhapadam samadiyama*), I resolve to train myself not to lie (*musavada veramani sikkhapadam samadiyama*), I resolve to train myself to refrain from alcohol and other drugs (*surameraya maja ppamadatthana veramani sikkhapadam samadiyama*).

14. In the Indian caste system, a Brahman is someone born in the caste of priests and hence "noble spirited," but in Buddhism this wording is used to indicate a *arhat*, someone who has attained enlightenment.

13. In the time of the Buddha, India was called Jambudipa (*jambu* translates as "forest") and was divided into 16 districts. The area where the Buddha was traveling around to share his teachings is called Majjhimadesa, the Middle-Earth, the "homeland" for Buddhists.

15. Reed-water village.

16. Demons, devilish men. *Yakkha* is also a general denomination of a nonhuman spirit, not necessarily evil, who lives in trees and in open spaces in forests. Altars were erected for them, and villagers would make burnt offerings there in exchange for favors and protective influences.

17. The Jewels, or *Ratana-sasana*, are the Buddha, the Dhamma (teaching), and the Sangha (community).

18. *Patimokkha* – the rules for monks, which were recited on full moon and new moon days in the community of fully initiated monks. There are 227 *patimokkha* rules for monks, and for nuns there are 311.

19. This is the original Pali version. In other translations (e.g. Lord Chalmers'), on the spot he had the nugget divided in four first, and then brought it to his home, which is a more plausible story.

20. The Non-returnee's Fruition (*anagami magga*, "they will not have to return in another life on earth") is the third path of the "four supernatural paths," by which the Buddhist cuts the two ties of sense and passion.

21. Literally: place of residence; probably here it refers to the personal living quarters.

22. Morals, virtues.

23. The *Maha-vagga* of the *Samyutta-Nikaya*, the Hawk Sutta.

24. Literally: "the killer"; "bringer of death," or *Namuci* (meaning: "the not-liberator," or the opposite of liberation). In Buddhist literature, Mara the Evil One (*papima maro*) is personified as "passion," "temptation," "seducer," or "evil."

25. One of the previous enlightened Buddhas.

26. Wisdom (*pañña*), moral or ethical behavior (*sila*); higher consciousness (*samadhi*). Here portrayed as unselfishness (altruism), morality, and belief (trust).

27. The *naga* was a mythological snake (cobra), capable of taking a human form.

28. This belief in substitute mercy is a perspective that was adopted only in later days; in the first foundations of the religion this was not so.

29. King of the gods or devas in the *Tavatimsa* heaven (heaven of the Thirty-Three). One of six heavens of the sphere of senses; *kamavacara* (or *kama loka*) is the sphere in which we are living. Here the Buddha preached the *Abhidhamma* (the Higher Teachings) until his mother, who died seven days after Sid-

dhartha was born, was reborn in the *Tusita* heaven as a man. She (or he) came to the *Tavatimsa* heaven to listen to the teachings. It is also in the *Tavatimsa* heaven where the Buddha stayed before he descended to this world, and where, according to the Buddhists, the future Buddha, *Metteyya* (Maitreya) resides.

30. See jataka 25.
31. Compare this story with the ethically much more high-minded one of the *Guttila Jataka* (number 25).
32. *Attha* or *artha*, meaning prosperity, happiness and well-being; compare with jataka 15.
33. Yama – the god of death.
34. Literally, baskets; meaning the canonic affirmations of the Buddha. It is not the only time these tales refer to them, but the references are a bit anachronistic because in the days of the Bodhisattva, the not-yet-enlightened Buddha, these scriptures did not even exist.
35. It is interesting to see that apparently in those days the number of inhabitants of Benares (Varanasi) was around 10,000 (probably including the country folk), while nowadays Benares has more than 800,000 inhabitants, with in additional 150,000 pilgrims daily, in an area of 47 square miles!
36. "Stories of the Residences," a book in the Buddhist Pali Canon.
37. Discourse, course of lectures.
38. Someone who has reached enlightenment and the highest grade of holiness. The liberation of the mind is the same as that of the Buddha, but there is a difference. The Buddha is also an arahat, but an arahat is not necessarily a Buddha. The difference is that the Buddha does not need a teacher who taught him the way to arahat-hood, but he himself discovered this way. It is true the arahat who is a pupil of the Buddha has reached enlightenment by his own effort, but with the aid of the tuition of a Buddha.
39. *Dhamma nupassana* is the fourth part of the *satipatthana* training. *Dhamma nupassana* means observation of things

like thoughts concerning the *Dhamma* (*cetasika dhamma*): obstacles like *kamacchanda, vyapada,* etc. (*nivarana*), the aggregates like *rupa, vedana,* etc. (*khandha*), sensory perception (*ayatanadhamma*), the factors of enlightenment like *sati, dhamma vicaya,* etc. *(bojjangadhamma),* and the Four Noble Truths (*Cattari Ariya Sacca*). This meditation can be considered as the most difficult in the *satipatthana* meditation series.

40. Also named the six unanimous monks, *Cha-bbaggiya.*

41. See also jataka 32.

42. Jujube berries (*Ziziphus jujuba*), from which a cough mixture is prepared.

43. The king is Gautama's well-known protector and disciple, the *Pasenadi* of Kosala.

44. The Ariya of the one who realizes the path of the "One who has entered the stream" (*sotapatti magga*).

45. See note 12.

46. Was initiated as a Buddhist monk.

47. In India it was common for a man, after 50 years or so of being a devoted husband, to leave the world in order to devote himself completely to the spiritual world, becoming a monk or an initiate of a guru.

48. *Kin-nara* – usually translated as "fairy" or "elf."

49. Sword, spear, bow and arrow, battle-axe and shield.

50. Domicile of the monks. See also jataka 21.

51. In some versions here follows a paragraph about how she owed her extreme beauty to her good deeds in a previous life.

52. If you try to calculate these proportions, you will get a very peculiar size of an elephant, but, ah well, it is a tale!

53. *Samyutta Nikaya* – related collections of scriptures, existing next to the *Ti Pitaka,* the three "hampers," or "baskets." The Buddhist Pali Canon containing all texts. It consists of three main sections: 1. rules (*Vinaya Pitaka*); 2. discourses (*Sutta Pitaka*); and 3. Higher Doctrine (*Abhidhamma*).

54. Damar trees (*Shorea robusta*).

55. Psalms from the *Theragatha,* the verses of the monks.

Other Publications from Binkey Kok

Ben Meulenbeld
Buddhist Symbolism in Tibetan Thangkas
Buddhism explained through contemporary Nepalese thangka paintings

Dirk Schellberg
Didgeridoo
Origins – how to make & play – musicians

Töm Klöwer
The Joy of Drumming
How to pick a percussion instrument and play—a complete handbook

Anneke Huyser
Singing Bowl Exercises for Personal Harmony
Relaxation, sound massage, chakra meditation

Kim-Anh Lim
Practical Guide to the I Ching
Down-to-earth interpretation of the ancient Chinese oracle known as the I Ching

Anneke Huyser
Mandala Workbook
Origins and forms of mandalas and how to make them for self-exploration

Harmonic Overtones
Book & CD
Magical vibrations in voice and music

Rainer Tillmann (Music), Dick de Ruiter (Text)
Crystal Sound
Book & CD
Explores the healing and tonal effects of crystal singing bowls,

which have a completely different resonance and effect than the Tibetan metal singing bowls.

Barramundi
Didgeridoo, Music for Meditation
Book& CD
Meditative but powerful sounds of the Australian wonder instrument

Irene Pool & Vincent Vrolijk
The Healing Sounds of Didgeridoo
Book& CD
An invitation to a personal spiritual journey

Nana Nauwald
Flying with Shamans
In Fairy Tales and Myths

Daniel Perret
Sound Healing with the Five Elements
Sound Instruments, Sound Therapy, Sound Energy

Dick de Ruiter
Hindu Folk Tales
From Ancient Ceylon